PORTRAIT OF A LANDSCAPE

BY DANIEL D. WATKINS

Glengoth
The Malcotte Worms
Malcotte Hall
Where Are the Songs of Spring?

Daniel Watkins was born in 1963 in Oxford and educated at Cambridge University where he studied Philosophy. He has written five novels including *Glengoth* and *Where Are the Songs of Spring?* which won finalist medals in the Next Generation Indie Book Awards, 2012 and 2013, respectively. He is an independent author and lives in Saudi Arabia and central Portugal.

PORTRAIT OF A LANDSCAPE

DANIEL D. WATKINS

PORTRAIT OF A LANDSCAPE

A NOVEL

BARESKINDIE
PEDRÓGÃO GRANDE

www.bareskindie.com
BARESKINDIE PAPERBACK EDITION

A CIP catalogue record for this title is available from the British Library.

ISBN: 1484979117
ISBN-13: 9781484979112

First Published in 2014 with
CreateSpace publishing platform

www.bareskindie.com

FOR

CLARE

Our whole guise is like giving a sign to the world to think of us in a certain way but there's a point between what you want people to know about you and what you can't help people knowing about you. And that has to do with what I've always called the gap between attention and effect.

Diane Arbus

AUTHOR'S NOTE

This is an art space, not a novel.

If you are reading this, you've just pushed through the glass doors and you're standing in the entrance hall, not sure if you want to spend too much time wandering the galleries. But it's raining outside and that's enough to convince you to wander over to the reception desk at least. Nothing better to do for now...

A good art exhibition is one in which the curator has considered the need to introduce their 'tenant' to a skeptical visitor. A good book is one in which the editor has likewise flagged concerns and, perhaps more than the author, cares that it might be read and even appreciated, for whatever reason. Many thanks to my editor – Heather Saunders – for her translation from British to American English and her concern that, my being the parent of this waif of a novel, I should provide some guidance, if only to protect an innocent child from an indifferent world. So, here's a note of sorts stuffed down the side of the cot left on the front steps of an orphanage.

The central location in the book is St. Ives in Cornwall (not New York). And, in part, the novel pays homage to the British artist and writer, Sven Berlin. If I am the father of this offspring of a work, then the mother text must be Sven Berlin's autobiographical 'novel', *The Dark Monarch*. Berlin's critical account of the St. Ives art colony in the 1950s was regarded by the various thinly fictionalized artists to be less portrayal than betrayal and, consequently, the author found himself sued for libel. Although back in print now with Finishing Publications, the book was pulped within weeks of publication in 1962.

A few words are perhaps needed on St. Ives and I am persuaded by Ms. Saunders that the postwar art colony in Cornwall is obscure enough, at least to a potential American readership, to warrant an apologia of elucidation. Actually, St. Ives had been attracting creative heavyweights decades before it became a bolthole for artists fleeing from Europe and London during, and a decade after, the Second World War. D.H. Lawrence lived in Zennor just outside St. Ives and Virginia Woolf was a visitor; her novel, *To the Lighthouse* was based on the lighthouse in Gwithian, round the bay from the town. But it is as an artists' colony that St. Ives is best known.

It would be condescending of me to explain who Barbara Hepworth was, or Ben Nicholson, though readers unfamiliar with these artists are encouraged to acquaint themselves with some awareness of their marriage and of Hepworth's better known sculptures inspired by weathered rocks and the moors with their Neolithic legacy of stone circles and monoliths from a lost age. Less important, perhaps, are Alfred Wallis or Patrick Heron or Peter Lanyon. These artists have, of course, been exhibited in New York and are well known enough to an intended audience for me to feel that they need no further introduction.

The novel abounds, of course, with other artists, including Damien Hirst, Saul Leiter, Tim Schmalz, Fritz Koenig, Jack Vettriano, Banksy, Andrea Verrocchio, Annie Leibovitz, Saul Steinberg, Arne Jacobson, Paul Gauguin, David Jones, Motonaga Sadamasa, Jiro Yoshihara, Bernard Leach, Matisse, Picasso, Leonardo da Vinci, Rembrandt, and groups such as Gutai, YBA, and Stuckists. In this age of digital information, the reader can easily explore these references and I would warmly recommend this because the work comes to life and deepens with awareness of them.

I wanted *Portrait of a Landscape* to be essentially a visual experience. By way of an encouragement to this effect, I have included six images for the main sections of the book. The reader is invited to consider their relevance and importance. All image references are intertwined with the narrative meanings of the novel. Again, I thank Heather

Saunders for some of her suggestions here. I should say that all the other artists, including Sara Choixu, are fictional.

I want to add a word about family. The marriage-children-separation-divorce 'story' that does lie like a thread of sorts between the frames of the book is, of course, the social world we live in. It is the world of the ordinary, the domestic, the trapped, and the closeted, whether of family and friends or artists' colony. Through Jack Rockshaw and Hugh Borne, I wanted to explore my own experience of coping with the timeless struggle between self and other, between individualism and the need for love that ties a knot in what it is to be human and to be creative.

Many thanks to Dr. Sophie Bowness, granddaughter of Dame Barabara Hepworth, for granting permission to include Hepworth's *Green Man,* 1972. I am also grateful to Dr. Anselm Kuhn, Director of Finishing Publications Ltd., for allowing the inclusion of Sven Berlin's illustration from *The Dark Monarch* along with an extract from the same work. Thanks to Tim Schmalz for allowing me to include the image of his sculpture, *Jesus the Homeless* and to Bryan Sargent for his photograph of Fritz Koenig's *Sphere.* Finally, I am very grateful to Clovis Henri Gauguin, grandson of Paul Gauguin, for granting permission to include his *Beetle with Imbeciles,* 2001.

August 2013

Pedrógão Grande

GREEN MAN, 1972
BARBARA HEPWORTH

OCTOBER

1

Jack Rockshaw now lay outside the frame of his world. Of his marriage. Everything that defined him was over *there* to one side; and the hotel room, the bed, the student lying asleep with the faint silk glow of her back to him, the wail of police sirens between the far-off chasms were now hiding him beyond the lens of his life. It was a place of the subconscious, unbounded and free of artifice. At least, that is what he tried to convince himself of as he listened to Amy's soft breathing. Jack yawned but was wide awake. It would be eight o'clock in Cornwall. Time to get up.

The thought of having to lay another five hours in wait for the sun to catch him pressed against his temples, and his eyes felt heavy. As he tried to doze, there was a vague, perhaps far-off sense that he hadn't escaped beyond the edge of things into a world behind the mirror, the landscape beyond the peripheral vision of his other life, but had simply landed in another picture. We slipped from one framed existence to another, blurred to begin with, maybe, but soon as focused and composed and determined as the old. No one lived in the spaces between, the borders, the meaningless wall-spaces not covered by landscapes or portraits. There was a photo of him with Elise and the kids and there was another of *this*. The two pictures were mounted side by side, one commenting on the other, not least of all because his image appeared in both. Just him. Frowning in one and smiling in the other in that ageless narrative sequence on the gallery wall: marriage and infidelity. What would a visitor feel, looking at him displayed up there for all to see? Amused? Sad? Disdainful? All responses would be conventional, culture-determined. And what would *he* feel, standing looking at the mirror of such a work? Jack closed his eyes. His sense of liberation was melting into the darkness.

"Jack?"

Amy's sleepy whisper brought him back from dozing off. He sensed her hand reaching out beneath the sheets. The distraction came from nowhere: a life buoy. He pushed himself over and cupped her shoulder in his hand. It was so delicate, like a bird's wing, but he felt the weight of her body gently transported into the tendons of his wrist, the muscles of his forearm as he lifted her round. She was listless with sleep at first, before her hand rose and reached deeper, her fingers curling tightly round before the nails impressed themselves.

"Mmm. You're awake."

"Amy?"

"Hmm? Oh, you really *are* awake!"

Amy shifted herself closer and didn't seem in the mood for conversation. Jack felt her greedy fingers, and his own mind melted into the darkness. Was this the liberation – sort of letting go of it all? Well then, God bless the night.

Amy was sinking down the bed.

"Amy?"

"Hmm?" An arm snaked up over his chest. A tentacle fingered up to his lips.

"Amy, I'm going to become nocturnal. I don't want to be defined by the day anymore. And . . . and when the sun rises, leave me here to sleep. I'll wait for –"

"Shh."

• • •

Are you free?

It was Elise. Hugh scrolled down the text message for more, but there was nothing. He sighed and looked across the studio, before glancing at his watch. He didn't want to talk. He didn't have to answer. But the familiar ring alarm started on his iPad before he had time to resolve himself into any sort of defiance and he felt the distant presence of Elise sitting down there in St. Ives, perhaps a little bored, a little insistent, the sea beyond Zennor framed azure behind her.

Hugh rose from his chair with an inaudible groan and made his way across the studio. His iPad was propped against a piece of board on an easel. When he got there, he leaned forward to press the screen. The ringing stopped and Elise's face appeared. She squinted back. She smiled abruptly.

"Did I disturb you? I'm sorry." She frowned. "You okay?"

"Let me get my chair."

Elise didn't reply and Hugh felt her concerned eyes on him as he turned away. He sensed his own curtness and felt bad all of a sudden. He glanced back over his shoulder.

"Looks sunny down there. Last of the autumn here," he offered.

There was no answer. Perhaps the connection wasn't so good.

Hugh picked up the director's chair and carried it back by the arms. He plonked it down and shifted round before peering at the screen.

"You still there?" he asked, turning himself and sinking carefully.

The woman in the picture nodded. They sat facing each other a little awkwardly, and Hugh found himself reading her face like he did. She flinched self-consciously and looked away.

"I was worried about you. Is everything okay?" she asked.

Hugh nodded and gave her a resigned look. He shrugged.

"Elise, I've been thinking. Maybe I should come when Jack gets back from New York." He sighed and glanced down at his hands. "And I need some time to myself." He looked back up and into those deep, brown, searching eyes. "It's been difficult since Marianne left. And Michael . . ." Hugh trailed off to check the reality of his emotions. "I don't know. I just need a break."

There was a pause and Hugh felt he should say more, but Elise cleared her throat.

"Okay. I understand. Jack was hoping to see you before he left," she said.

Hugh could tell she was trying her best not to sound disappointed in any way that would pressure him. He melted a little at her kindness, and whatever determination he had prepared began to blur.

"Sure."

"We're here, Hugh. Jack will miss you. I don't know when he'll get back. It's a bit open-ended. I thought you wanted the winter –"

"I do. Elise, I really want to do this. I need to." Hugh shook his head. "It's a focus thing. I can't connect to the Pieta. You know?"

He looked beseechingly at Elise, who stared back with concern.

"I don't know what you want me to say, Hugh. I mean, I think you should come down like we all planned. Find the time down here. Staying in London's not going to help.

Hugh winced. He glanced over the top of the easel to the metal-framed window in the far white wall. The clinker-gray London brick of the building across the narrow way blanked back at him.

"Hugh?"

"I know. You're right." He lowered his eyes and tried to smile. "I need time and space." He felt suddenly a little annoyed. "Look, can I think a bit about this? I mean, of course I'll come, but I haven't yet decided that I will. I can't explain. I need to determine what I'll do next, not just drift." He felt the annoyance intensify and define itself. He shook his head and leaned away from the easel. "I've drifted for years. Look where it's gotten me. I'm fucked off with the decadence of it."

There was a moment's silence. Hugh looked back at Elise framed and waiting. Watching him from Cornwall.

"I'm sorry," he said. "I'm half talking to myself again. Be patient with me, Elise. Let me feel I'm making the decision. Can you do that for me?"

Hugh looked at Elise cautiously. Had he said something that would upset her? She carried her altruisms with such a sensitive pride.

"Sure." She gave him a maternal caress of a smile. "I understand. Look, the barn is ready. The stone will be arriving next week." She lowered her eyes as if something in her lap had distracted her. "It's all good."

"Yes."

"Aren't you excited?" she said quietly, raising her head to look into him. Hugh blinked back stupidly. Her question had taken him off guard. There was so much else going on.

"Excited?" He shrugged. "It's a commission. Commerce kills creativity. I'm frightened by it maybe. I have to bring something of myself to it all. If I can't, it'll be shit for money like everything else. Who cares?"

He sensed Elise shift awkwardly.

"Well, go and sort yourself out, Hugh. Get a nice lunch. Sit in the pub. I don't know. Okay. Hugh?"

"What? Yes –"

"We're here. Everything's here waiting for you."

"I know. Thank you. Thank you for everything."

• • •

The low autumn sun painted the trees along Grange Road. Hugh Borne felt the faint warmth on the back of his head as he turned into Bermondsey Street. Elise and Cornwall were still very much in his mind. He pictured himself as a tiny figure heading west and turning north as if he was in a Steinberg Ninth Avenue cartoon but with the Atlantic, not Pacific, on the horizon, and Dorset and Devon, rather than Jersey and Nebraska, closer to. As he walked on, the windowed walls of Bermondsey Square blocked the sunlight. How the city hemmed him in: each building was a hand held up to shade and enclose, each glimpsed vista was a landscape shaved into a narrow portrait to entice and frustrate the curious eye. He crossed the road and headed on past St. Mary's. It was still quite early and a few joggers ran the other way down the middle of the quiet Sunday morning street.

No. It wasn't that he drifted. It was that he allowed other people to make the decisions for him. Hugh stopped and looked back. The joggers were turning left into Abbey Street. He caught the precise moment they disappeared: a trainer cut from view by dark brick. It was as if they had been eaten. Marianne had acted decisively. Not for him, but for herself. For a second, he almost saw how he must appear to others. It was so difficult. Like trying to see the back of your head in a mirror. Marianne had the key to his other self that remained hidden to him and she had waved it triumphantly to taunt and mock that she knew the real Hugh Borne; what he thought was his social persona was the real him and he was too blind to see that he was a tiresome, self-absorbed bore. No one could live with such a narcissist. Everyone felt sorry for her. The words, the fights bubbled up again and he closed his eyes as if seeing was hearing. He opened them again and turned to carry on, suddenly thirsty for distraction.

Yes. The triumph of the will was not to act but to see. If he couldn't perceive himself, he at least could perceive Marianne. We all saw others more easily than ourselves. Marriage had been ridiculous: not a binding through exchanged vows but through exchanged keys. Marianne had waved his in that mocking, angry way. He had just held hers passive and curious at a woman who didn't know who she was.

He was nearly there: the café with the plate glass façade. People looking out. People looking in, or rather, at themselves reflected. Such wonderful mirrors where there were pools of shadow or darkness within that caught you better looking than you actually were. Hugh smiled to himself. Was he *really* narcissistic? But he always preferred to sit on the inside looking out, counting the people who glanced at themselves and caught the corner of his eye – women mainly. There was a chair in the window now. If he acted decisively, he'd get a ringside seat.

Coffee. Hugh pushed the door and the aroma unbuttoned the shirt of his senses. There was a slightly seductive warmth and then the sharp hissing of a milk steamer frothing up. A tamping down of espresso grains. The combination pulled him to the counter. Elise's last comment wandered by, the one about going off to a pub for a beer or something. Hugh glanced around. There were tatty design magazines scattered over side tables and a beat-up sofa. Pub? He wasn't a real heavy drinker. Elise liked her wine though. She had been pretty wild at Falmouth. How strange that they had all been squeezed into this middle life, tamed, boxed, and shipped off into the sexless functionality of marriage, kids, affairs, and divorce.

"You all right?"

Hugh turned round at the voice. Friendly. Like a student working weekends.

"Sorry. Yeah. Um, I'll have a cappuccino," he replied.

"Large or regular?" It was a girl. She spoke with her back to him, already busy at the machine. Hugh hesitated and she glanced around.

"I don't know. Large, I guess."

"Large? Chocolate on top?"

"Sure. Why not. Yes, thanks."

The girl turned completely round to face him. She wiped a hand on her apron and turned the key on the register. Another machine. Her movements were automated.

"£2.69. Anything else?"

Anything else? Everything else. Anything other than this 'else'.

The girl turned back for his cappuccino and lifted it round. She pushed the mug across the counter at him, avoiding eye contact.

"No. That's fine. Thanks."

Hugh took the coffee and moved away. The window seat was still free but people were beginning to come in and he felt his legs jerk into more purposeful action. This was London: a seat free for a second then gone. How many little defeats and failures could a man screw into himself? Elise was right, maybe. He should leave London sooner. To stay indoors was to be haunted by the pain of it all. To go outside was to be hunted; you couldn't stop on the pavement without someone bumping into you.

"Oh, sorry."

"Sorry?"

Hugh turned round as he was about to sit down. A girl had knocked his elbow and there was a neat brown splat of coffee and foam on the floorboards. A drop or two caught the side of his shoe. Hugh felt he must have been staring down too long. The girl had already opened the glass door and had gone out. The door closed again and he shrugged. Why did he keep seeing women? It was like some sort of joke. Disconcerting, as if they had been written into some life narrative to make a point. What. About him? His narcissism? The vanity of a moderately acclaimed artist? The arrogance of a creative man hated by an ex-wife for all that? Yes.

Hugh sank slowly onto the black vinyl chair. Seventies retro. Arne Jacobson. Bloody awkward and, as he shifted himself to be more comfortable, uncomfortable. He looked at his cappuccino, now miles away, like his life – this time denied him by a fucking chair. He sighed inaudibly to himself and sat like a resigned chick too weak to be bothered with the shell of it all. The girl was there. She'd gone out for a puff. A bag of blue smoke billowed past the window and she was yacking at someone he couldn't see beyond the frame and the wall. She had her skinny right elbow cupped in her left hand, hips slouched, high-arched wrist hooked over her cigarette. Elegant and uncouth all in one.

2

Michael Borne emerged from the rectangular cave of the Sloane Square tube station and stood in a pool of autumn sunshine. The air was cold. The trees in the square were sharp orange and tipped with bright yellow against a plate of dark lapis lazuli. The teenager winced at the vibrancy of it all like a sobering drunk. And he recoiled. For a moment, it looked as if he might turn tail and head back underground. Instead, he took a hesitant step, turned right, and wandered a little, before performing a one-eighty to carry on, seemingly with more purpose. But he was walking away. He crossed the road and into the square, now heading toward Peter Jones' department store farther off. His destination was a restaurant just a hundred yards from the station but he'd take the square clockwise, the long way round, because he wasn't ready to see his father for the last time – at least, that was how it seemed. The pain was not because this felt like a farewell, but because he didn't want to see his father. As he shambled on around the ring, he was filled with the anger of a teenager too fresh and raw for analysis. He didn't want it to be picked over. He didn't know how the fact that his father would try to unpack his feelings just upset him more. Everything was unconscious: an inner experience only visible from the outside. He was going to be exposed and the shame just boiled into a fist.

Michael didn't have the adult's toolkit for making sense of things. He didn't have the device for rewinding the past to play over the bits he had missed. Instead, for the last month or so, the present moment seemed to have come out of nowhere. Beyond the anger and a vague sense of betrayal, lay a deep anxiety that things didn't make sense. His mental construct of the world was all askew.

Michael could see the restaurant skulking through the trees on the corner of Sedding Street. It was a favorite of his father's, which just made things worse. The storm of fights and shouting, slamming doors, cars driving off in the night, and his mother's epic phone calls, had all come out of nowhere. The fact that his parents' marriage had been spiraling downwards for years had eluded him completely.

The restaurant was already busy. Most of the tables had been taken. The waitress glanced around for him. There. Michael looked over to the far wall, his father instantly recognizable: a stranger framed by a fish, a bird, and a squid. There was a black bug that looked like a scarab, or maybe it was a stag beetle. He'd seen the animals and plants painted on the wall before and they were more familiar than the man now rising from the white bench seat behind the table. The waitress smiled.

"Okay? I'll be with you in a moment. Can I take your coat?"

Michael felt awkward. He wanted to smile back but he shook his head instead and, anyway, the waitress was already turning to deal with another customer. Unescorted, Michael stepped reluctantly through the restaurant. When he reached the table under the mural, he didn't see that his father saw his angst. He didn't understand that was why Dad fumbled his words as he sat back down and away. Something about the weather.

Michael began to remove his jacket. The waitress came over as he pulled his chair back and went to sit down. There was a middle-aged couple at the neighboring table like an audience that had been invited to sit on the stage. Michael didn't know where to look, so he fixed his eyes on the beetle as he sat and pulled his chair forward. The waitress was handing him a menu over his left shoulder.

"Anything to drink?"

There was a pause for an answer.

"Michael?"

"Coke please. Thanks."

"Okay, one Coke. With ice and lemon?" asked the waitress.

"Um. No. I mean, just ice. Thanks."

"Okay. And sir?"

Mr. Borne inhaled deeply for inspiration. He touched his brow with a forefinger.

"Glass of, um, Le Cadet."

"Lussac-Saint Emilion. That's lovely. Okay. Be back with you in just a moment."

Michael sensed her remove something from the table. Maybe it was a wine glass. She left them. He coughed and waited for his father to begin. There was an interesting curly design on the forks. He saw it was repeated on the knife handles and the spoons too.

"Michael? Thanks for coming. I thought you . . ." His father's voice faltered. "Well, I know this wasn't easy for you. I just wanted –"

"Dad, it's okay." Michael peered to his right. It was okay. The couple at the next table was getting stuck into themselves. They were happy to be together. Distracted well enough. Michael felt sufficiently brave to continue. "I just don't want to talk about it."

"About what?"

Michael didn't know how to answer. He didn't want to talk about anything. He didn't even want to be here. His father shifted.

"I'm leaving London for a while. I've got some work in St. Ives. A friend. The Pieta. I'm staying with the Rockshaws. Remember them?"

Michael let his eyes drift up from the cutlery. His father was wearing a blue shirt open at the neck by three buttons. That black corduroy jacket with the elbow patches. Dressed for a woman. A friend.

"That's nice."

"Your mother and I spoke about Paris. I'm happy for you to go. I think you should go. We all need to get out of London."

"Sure."

"I'll be away all winter."

Michael frowned imperceptibly at some vague realization that was too hurtful. He heard his father sigh.

"But your school. You'll make new friends there. It's what your mother wanted. You'll get to see your French cousins. Amelie is at the

British School. You met her once. She's a lovely girl. Maybe a year older than you, I think."

"I was two."

There was a moment's silence.

His father was about to speak. Something in the pause made Michael brace himself for the opening cliché: Your mother and I . . . It would be the cue for him to rise and leave. The threat hovered over them like the sword of Damocles. His mother and father had nothing. There *was* no 'both' somehow going on behind the façade of loathing, as if everything about his parents' marriage had been magically reversed. He shouldn't be forced to play the parent over two squabbling brats like this. He felt so ashamed of them. He'd given birth to a couple of shits.

"Wine and Coke?"

The waitress had rather miraculously turned into a waiter. Michael looked up. He was a little disappointed. He was increasingly desperate to latch on to people. Strangers. Anyone. But this guy didn't make eye contact. The man looked bored. Indifferent. Stupid. Anyway, Michael didn't like men. Men were arse holes.

"Er, Coke," his dad said looking at him.

"You ready to order?" the waiter asked.

Michael looked up at the squid. The waiter hovered.

"Sorry. Not yet. We need a bit more time."

"Sure. No worries."

The guy was Australian. *No worries*? Michael winced.

The waiter disappeared after passing over the wine, and the Coke now sat on the table at his elbow. Red plastic straw. A slice of lemon.

"Right. We'd better look at the menu," he heard his father announce, as if it was a chore. It was a chore.

Looking at the menus together was agony.

"What are you having? Did you want a starter?"

Michael shook his head. He didn't know what he wanted. He didn't care.

"What's steak tartare?" he asked.

"You don't want that. It's raw meat."

Michael looked up and caught his dad's face for the first time. He scanned his father with critical eyes, as a woman might. There was too much skin. Gray hair. Lines carved with a knife. *How could any woman find –*

"Here. Why don't you try the Longhorn beef burger? Eight ounces."

His father was reading from the menu. Scanning the options for him. Instead of him. Michael closed his eyes and leaned back. He shrugged and felt a surge of rebelliousness.

"It's all right. I want to try it. The raw one."

His father looked up. Michael didn't see him frown and lower the menu.

"Well, okay. If you're sure. It's French. Plenty of that sort of thing in Paris. So . . . I'll have the bavette. There." The menu was closed. "Would you like a glass of wine?" His father was already looking out over his head for the waiter.

"No thanks."

His father wasn't listening. He raised his hand.

"Waiter." He had caught the Australian's eye and was nodding. Michael felt his dad had become impatient, as though he wanted to get this whole thing over and done with. The subtle realization broke inside him. He felt suddenly tearful. He breathed in deeply and hunched his shoulders a little.

"Ready to order?" Michael heard the waiter. He was now standing at the side of the table.

"Yes. I'll have the steak bavette. And, er, steak tartare."

"How'd you like your steak?"

"Medium. Um, no. Rare."

"Rare?"

"Rare."

The waiter leaned over and took the menus.

Michael felt his dad eyeing him.

"It's good to try out different things. New things. Always embrace change."

What was his father going on about?

"We get too complacent. Stuck into routines. Same choices."

Michael cleared his throat. He looked at his glass of Coke.

"I'm going to miss you. Michael?"

Michael shifted uneasily and went to lift his glass.

His dad sighed and gave up trying for a bit. Michael lifted the glass and took a sip, pushing the straw to one side, and drinking like an adult not a dumb kid. The slice of lemon nudged his top lip annoyingly. He hated lemon. There was a faint waxy aroma insipid against the sharp fizz of bubbles sprinkling against the end of his nose. Perhaps he should have used the straw.

"Michael?"

"I'm listening."

He heard his father cough nervously. It was for something like a confession. He felt his father leaning forward.

"Look, Michael. It's difficult. I know what . . . look, I don't know what your mother has been telling you but . . . well, I didn't let her down. It didn't happen like that. Life's complicated. When you're older you'll understand. You'll see."

• • •

Through the restaurant's plate glass window – defined by a gray awning, rusticated Portland stone, the narrow pavement – a waiter was bringing two plates to a table against the wall. Below the cliffs of the reflected buildings across the street and over the tops of a shoal of passing cars, two customers were rising from their seats, as the waiter – plates held high and hovering – treaded the water. There was a boy taking his coat from the back of a chair. The man was talking. He held out his hands but the boy floated silently away on the tide of the tables.

3

The sickle of cream cut the gray-green sea. The white lighthouse at Gwithian – Virginia Woolf's lighthouse – disappeared behind the serge of gorse bushes, then the dunes beyond the golf course at Lelant. The raindrops on the gray carriage window wobbled rhythmically to the movement of the train now trundling toward the rocks and battered palms below Carbis Bay. Hugh wondered which artists' eyes had shared this view. His vision. Hepworth and Nicholson perhaps? Or had they come down by car?

The bay of St. Ives was suddenly cut off by the rising tide of land.

Hugh turned away from the window. He had been to St. Ives a couple of times before. Once with Marianne, when Michael was about five. They had come down to see the Rockshaws for a week's holiday. Jack had been a godsend. Held everything together. The other time had been for work. Must have been shortly after the Tate first opened. They had wanted some of his animal pieces for the Primitives exhibition. But St. Ives wasn't a town you returned to easily. It had always been a place for refuge. Exile. Jack was Cornish. His family was from St. Agnes. Maybe that was how he had held things together so well that summer, when the 'foreigners' were falling apart. He was seldom off home turf these days. If New York wasn't also a repository of uprooted souls, he'd be having a tough time of it. The thought of Jack being away left Hugh suddenly pining for the city. Leaving London was a withdrawal not without symptoms.

Hugh felt himself tense. A sort of claustrophobia. Hepworth must have felt like this the first time down from London. Nicholson was an ice-cold solitary. He could live and work happily on the dark side of the moon. Hadn't he gone to Switzerland after all? But Barbara? A mother. God. It must have been a long day's journey into the night. The raging envy. In his own marriage, it was Marianne who had fled. He had known she would eventually cut and run, even before they had got married. She had been a Vivienne Haigh-Wood, a Sylvia Plath to Ted Hughes. His Fulvia. Planets pulled by colliding attraction toward mutual destruction: flirtation, coupledom, marriage.

• • •

"Do you remember the barn?"

"I remember the barn."

Elise stopped on the path up from the house. She looked at Hugh and he caught an almost gleeful spark in her eyes. She had always been mischievous. He must have looked a little unnerved. She turned to carry on and she smiled.

"I know you're worried. The stone arrives tomorrow, Hugh. Just maybe take a week off. Go for walks. Let the place sink into you. Winter's coming. You'll get the solitude you wanted. It'll drive you crazy." She laughed and leaned toward him.

The barn was next to Jack's studio and had been done up since he last saw it. Two white-framed windows had been knocked into its granite face so the building could now stare back at them. The Cornish slates had been repointed and sat tight and heavy against the Atlantic storms that would pile in over Gunard's Head and Treen. They glistened against the light drizzle, like silver sequins of cod. It wasn't the wreck of a barn he had imagined or remembered. And the main house seemed close by. It was cozy. Domestic. Suburban. Hugh began to feel he had made a dreadful mistake.

They had reached the door and Elise lifted the latch with a metallic echo that spoke of an emptiness, like within a church. She didn't open the door, but she looked at Hugh with a little concern, her right hand on the handle.

"Are you okay?"

"I'm fine."

"You don't like it."

Hugh frowned and shook his head unconvincingly.

"Of course I like it. Elise, I'm very grateful. You didn't have to do this. It's perfect. I mean, you and Jack have done so much."

"I know you don't like it. I can tell. We had it done up. Hugh, it was falling down."

Hugh sighed with feigned frustration.

"Elise. It's perfect. Come on. Let's look inside. I'm getting wet."

Elise looked up. The drizzle was intensifying. She pushed the door open and stepped back to let Hugh enter first.

"Please," she prompted.

Hugh stepped in and barely had time to take in the space: the whiteness of fresh paint, professional studio heaters, and perfect light, even on this gray autumn afternoon. Elise continued.

"I know it's not what you wanted."

Hugh turned to look at her. She was closing the door.

"Elise, it's wonderful."

"No. It's dull. Sanitized." She left the door and came up to him. She shrugged her shoulders. "I know. I'm sorry."

Hugh sighed.

"It's fine."

"I knew you would be disappointed. I mean, letting me persuade you to come down here. It's like I lied to you. Led you on."

She walked into the space and turned to face him.

"I did lie, Hugh. Really."

Hugh smiled and shook his head.

"You lied, did you?"

Elise nodded.

"Yes, I did. Because I know you're a romantic. You're a Sven Berlin. You're a sculptor. Everything has to be muscled out like gutting a stag. And look at this place. Nothing heroic is going to come out of here. It's a granny annex. An iPad."

She turned a full circle looking up at the honey-gold roof timbers and laughed.

"I'm a complete witch."

Hugh stared at her now standing facing him. Naughty and braced. He narrowed his eyes and sighed.

"Well Elise, you haven't changed at least. So, you tricked me, did you?" He shook his head and looked round. "Then I will defy you."

"Good."

"Yes."

• • •

Hugh drove Jack's car beyond Treen and took the left fork before Morvah like Elise had instructed. The lane narrowed into a track that took him south up onto the brown moors, the wide gray sea behind and beyond. He had set off early, before the school run into St. Ives. Elise said she needed to wait for some prints to arrive at the gallery and would be there after dropping the kids off. She'd be back home about lunch-time. Hugh knew she was giving him the space he craved. It was kind of her. She was no witch, but more of a pixie and, though not Cornish, Celtic and as capricious. She made him feel mentally cumbersome. Saxon-heavy and oversized. A Neanderthal tall among the Ebu Gogo.

It wasn't the Mên-an-Tol he had come to see, though he parked the car next to the wall and the track that led there. He had come for the Nine Maidens, a megalithic stone circle some way farther back to the east. He wanted to walk across the spongy heather and through the gorse and broom. He didn't mind the destruction of the barn if he could come out to this wedge of an island county seven miles across framed by the restless sea.

He knew he had to be careful not to go too far from the beaten paths. It was easy to get caught up in the barbed brambles and gorse bushes if you were too impatient to take the direct line. There could be great swathes of treacly bog.

The route he decided on took him past the 'crick' stone. He had wanted to avoid it but the path took him by. It was a growling dog of a memory. Some ten years ago, he had been there with Marianne and

Michael. There was a photo somewhere – lost now, of course – of Michael leaning out of the hollowed granite stone. It had been a bright blustery day in late June. The wind off the sea had blown a strand of Michael's fair hair across his eyes. He had crawled through to emerge squinting at the intensity of the day. Hugh now glanced at the tomb of a memory.

Hepworth must have brought the triplets to this now bleak place. It was a monument for mothers after all. Hole or whole? An emptiness or completeness? But it had already been captured and he wished, just briefly, he had thought of it first. Hugh had now stopped, against all his intentions, and found himself staring at the toll flanked by its two phallic stumps. This was nature. Man as nature monumented. Couldn't he also take the stone from the earth and plant it in his soul like some lithic tree? God damn her! She had stolen this place and stuck it on John Lewis's, the UN building, college gardens. He stood there, an archaeologist before a robbed grave.

The gold had gone. Hugh stepped away. He looked out to the east and felt the pull of his own purposed goal. Wasn't there enough on these ancient moors for other thieves? Good artists copied, great artists stole. Hugh smiled sadly and moved off.

• • •

The remaining stones of the Nine Maidens, gapped over the centuries by farmers for cowshed plinths and lintels, lay where they had plummeted from the heavens. The Pleiades, or some such constellation, fallen to earth. An anti-catasterism.

At first, Hugh stood in the center of the stone circle. There might still be a magical problem. How was this place to be defined? Were these stones or was this a circle? Here was a nothing defined by something. There was no hole without a ring. *Nothing* could be experienced, felt as *something*, when encircled like this. It was so simple. So plain. But this was not only what Hugh had come to witness. Here lay the imprint of the mind's first reconnection with its origins. This was the edge of the first tide that had left such stones as these scattered across the continents from the deserts of Jordan to the far western isles. Diurnal tombs of nocturnal stars. There would be other waves, always from the east heading west against the winds. But these rocks had been carried by the first flood of man's reaching out, left scattered and abandoned by the wadi's diaspora. Once, the gods had been heavenly bodies. Since the time where Hugh now stood, man had been falling steadily back to earth, pulled by the massy gravity of his own ego. If men had not become gods, gods had become men. Gravity had become so strong it was hard to raise one's head to look up and out at the anthropomorphism of it all.

Hugh peered at the low clouds crawling over the headland from the southwest. Was the woman who had been here before going to haunt him with her hollows? The witch of St. Ives. He felt the nine phallic sentinels watch with suspicion. How could he find inspiration from such a place when it had all been done before? This was a barren isle: gutted of its fish, scraped clean of its ore, and stripped of what little it could have offered to inspire. Nothing heroic was going to come out of this place, this experience. Hugh didn't feel haunted so much as hunted. He wouldn't be the first to have been chased out. All exiles were soon exiled. He heard the roar of the Lawrences caught in the wind across the gorse and the nightmare years at Tregerthen. Sven Berlin's Dark Monarch stalked the dead land. So many ghosts. With envy, Hugh pictured Jack asleep now in some hotel room in New York. He would wake in some hours' time to a warm glow of satisfaction at a transatlantic career and the gentle rumble of traffic from the caverns below.

God! It was with a sense of rising panic at the place that Hugh let the monoliths draw him away from the center of the circle like an upturned vessel on a Ouija board. Slowly and cautiously, he crossed the uneven ground. He felt the pull of one of the smaller and more upright stones. When he got close up, he could see it patched with ochre and silver lichen. The gray granite was rutted and pocked. There were splitters' scars down one side. Hugh closed his eyes and reached out with both hands to feel the sharp cold quartz with the ends of his fingers. Couldn't there be something left for him on these ancient bones picked clean?

4

She had been expecting the man from the quarry, so when she saw Hugh stride past the kitchen window – his stern face, the raincoat, the gray hair swept back – she felt a flash of confusion. He hadn't seen her standing there watching and now taking him in. Poor Orpheus. He was removing the back door key from his coat pocket, his eyes cast down. He was miles away. She chose not to call out or go over to open the door for him. Instead she went to turn the kettle on. She was glad the quarry people hadn't arrived. It would give the two of them some time to talk about things over a coffee.

There was no water in the kettle. The door from the porch opened suddenly. It made her jump.

"You're back. I'm just making coffee. Like some?"

Hugh looked up. A little surprise in his eyes at seeing her.

"Oh. Hi. I didn't know you were in."

"How'd it go?"

Hugh was already taking his coat off. She watched him as he moved to fold it over the back of a kitchen chair.

"What?"

"The stones. Did you –"

Elise stopped herself. She wasn't feeling a good vibe from Hugh. She went to the sink under the window and turned on the tap. The water filled a momentary silence between them.

"Coffee," she said affirmatively returning the kettle to boil.

"Sure. That'd be nice." There was a sigh in Hugh's flat response. "How was the gallery? Did the prints turn up?" He pulled out a chair from the kitchen table and made to sit down.

"Oh, Hugh. Boring stuff. Just nothing." Elise spoke as she put out two coffee mugs and a French press.

"Not boring. I want to see your work sometime."

Elise laughed. A coffee spoon tinkled thrown into a mug.

"Frames, Hugh. You don't need frames. Anyway, I want to hear about your morning."

She frowned to herself before glancing round at him. He was sitting hunched over the table. He looked so down. But she had two teenagers and it had become second nature for her to go wading in at times like this. She cleared her throat.

"Tell me. Tell me what happened."

Hugh began to shake his head but she persisted.

"No, you have to tell me everything. Just get it out."

"*Just*?"

"Hmm. *That* bad?" She ignored the irritation in his face.

Hugh groaned and leaned back with a stretch. He shook his head.

"You know, Elise, I can't do this anymore."

"Okay. Then don't."

The chair creaked and Hugh looked round at her half-astonished. Possibly hurt. Then he smiled and nodded.

"Sure. Then what I meant to say was I don't want to do this anymore. I mean . . . What do I mean?"

The kettle switch clicked and Elise turned from him.

"You're too impatient. You're just getting over a divorce and you've only just arrived." Elise pushed the press down on the grains as she spoke. "It will come to you. You won't find it on the moor going out like you're hunting rabbits." She lifted their mugs and brought the coffee things over to the table.

"I know. But I don't belong here. Nothing up there is going to come looking for me. I think I've got this whole commission horribly wrong. I mean, what I visualized, you know, with the local granite and the memories, the ghosts . . ." Hugh trailed off and looked at Elise, his eyes more animated. "They were all up there."

"Oh, biscuits. Fancy a biscuit? Who was up there?"

Elise got up from her chair.

"The whole Penwith lot. And the others. Lanyon floating around like a shitful seagull. Screams from the Lawrences. Mayhem. All after what? It was horrible. At first I heard the ancients. But they got drowned out. Hepworth stole them and stuffed them up Oxford Street."

Elise returned with a tin of biscuits.

"Now, now."

"Well. I mean. That's the whole point. We hover between some sort of ego manic, arrogant, wank we call art and the worst kind of capitalist kitsch for pigeons to shit on. It's all masturbation."

"I said you were a romantic. Milk's just there. "Hepworth had to pay the bills like everyone else."

"Yes. Precisely. There you are. God. I'm in a vice!" There was a sudden sharp pain in Hugh's voice. He screwed up his eyes.

Elise wasn't impressed. Her Orpheus was being a little too theatrical.

"Vice?" she probed out of politeness more than curiosity. Hugh leaned forward and opened his eyes.

"I need the money. I need the fucking money." He shook his head and laughed. He looked at her. "Sure, you're right. I'll do it again and see if I get away with it. Produce more shit."

Elise shrugged.

"Well. Do it that way. It's professional. I mean, isn't that work – to do what you don't want to do for money? That's what we all have to fill the days with."

Hugh stared blankly down at his coffee.

"I just hoped that now and again it was different. You know, that I could connect to what I was doing. Put something of myself into this project."

"Well, then give it time."

"I haven't got time. I've got to deliver in March."

"Oh, that reminds me. The stone should be arriving. Perhaps I should phone. See when they're coming."

She felt Hugh tense.

"Hugh, I don't need to give you lessons on how to do this. You've been here before. Over and over. It's what you do. Wrestle with it. I can't help you. Biscuit?"

Hugh shook his head and leaned away.

"No thanks."

He looked thoughtful and there was a silence between them before Hugh spoke slowly, deliberately as if he was trying to remember something.

"I was thinking of the cave paintings at Lascaux. On the way back."

"Ah yes. Have you been there?"

"I wish. It's closed now. They were getting damaged."

"Sure."

"But it got me thinking about, I don't know, primitivism, I suppose. You know, the whole Alfred Wallis thing. All children are artists."

"Wallis wasn't primitive, he was naïve. Anyway, Picasso was full of shit. Women are doormats or goddesses, blah, blah. Not sure where that leaves *me*. Too many artists think that just being able to paint gives them the right to spout crap. Like actors."

Hugh smiled. Elise felt that he was glad she was getting riled. Perhaps he didn't feel so lonely.

"Hmm. No fan of Picasso. I'd forgotten," he said, finally lifting his coffee.

"He was a libidinous goat."

Hugh narrowed his eyes at her.

"Okay, well. But the cave paintings. Those guys could really draw. The curves of the animals. You know what I mean?"

"What, and then there was Wallis and his cardboard boats."

Hugh nodded and raised his eyebrows.

"Precisely. It's a terrible word."

"What, naïve?"

"No. Primitive. You know. Colonial and all that. I mean, the stones. Up there on the moors. 'Primitive' is completely the wrong word. It's something to do with perception. And their perception was as sharp as ours. As intelligent. They weren't kids. Kids are basically stupid through ignorance. It's a disaster to somehow transpose the development of an individual from birth to maturity onto civilizations ancient to modern. Perceptions haven't changed. It's the worlds that have changed. Technologies, that's all. It's monstrous to take the world of up there then stick it on the wall of a shop in Central London. That's what I realized. That's why this commission is fucked."

"Oh. Well, it wasn't Hepworth's fault."

"What do you mean?"

"I mean, she just delivered the goods. She was pragmatic, I guess. In the end pragmatism underwrites all the isms."

"And I'm not?"

Elise smiled back.

"What? Pragmatic? You will be. You've got legal fees to pay."

Hugh nodded slowly. He sighed.

"That's what's changed. Money. We lost sight of the stars. We gained nothing."

"Do you want to cancel the order? I can phone the quarry."

Elise was being deliberately provocative. She had things to do and wanted to get on. Simon and Caja might need picking up from Truro.

Hugh shook his head. And looked down at his hands, now rested on the table next to his mug.

"See? I am in a vice."

Elise began to push her chair back.

"Your coffee's getting cold." She rose and touched Hugh's shoulder. "Look. I've been thinking too. We take what materials we have. We work within the perimeters that are set. Then we take a little bit of ourselves and somehow work that in. It's what women do all the time. We have more patience, maybe. Don't idealize the past and demonize the present. Now is where we've always had to live. Seriously, take a week off. Don't think about it. Talk to my kids. Get to know them. Maybe you need people, not stones to talk to. Talk to Jack later. He'll be video conferencing tonight."

Elise removed her hand and turned away.

"There's more coffee if you wanted."

"I wish I was in New York." Hugh leaned round. "Seriously. It never occurred to me."

Elise frowned, she felt slightly hurt. Maybe a little annoyed.

"Well, there are no Neolithic sites in Central Park that I know of. That's what you wanted, Hugh. Remember?"

He was behaving like a spoiled child.

"Look, maybe I should phone the quarry. We can't wait around all afternoon. I think I've got to go to Truro."

Hugh blinked at her as if coming out of a reverie.

"Don't worry, I can wait for the stone. I need to be here for that anyway."

Elise looked at him. She was emptying the coffee grains into the sink.

"Well, I suppose so. It's a bit annoying having to wait around like this."

"I thought you said women have patience."

"Ha ha. I'm impatient on your behalf, Hugh. That's another difference."

"What?"

Elise raised the coffee plunger in her hand and waved it slightly.

"Empathy."

Just then the phone rang. She lowered the French press and glanced at Hugh.

"I bet that's them."

Hugh got up from his chair and looked at the door.

"Shall I get it?"

Elise was already wiping her hands on a tea towel. She shook her head.

"It's okay. Might be the kids."

She smiled at Hugh and swept past. She felt his excitement. Women *were* more empathetic. She felt the confirmation of the fact as she hurried out. She sensed Hugh loiter a little impotently behind before following.

The phone was in the hall near the front door. Elise picked up the handset and looked at Hugh as he stepped through from the kitchen.

"Hello?" She looked up at Hugh and then nodded. It was them. "Yes. It is. Yes. Mrs. Rockshaw. Yes? Oh. Oh I see. That's a shame." Elise looked at Hugh rolling his eyes and shaking his head. "Tomorrow?"

Hugh was shaking his head with annoyance. She shrugged back.

"Okay, well look, we can't hang around like today. Can't you phone by nine or something to say you're coming?"

Hugh nodded. She nodded back.

"Okay. Well thanks for ringing anyway. Goodbye."

She lowered the handset and hung up.

5

It was good to be on the surf if only to get out of the house. But even along the west end of Porthmeor, near the rocky headland, the waves were mushy and closed-out. The October wind was blustery and a little onshore. The cold made Jonah yawn. His jaw ached from shivering. There was one other guy up toward the Mount. No one he knew. A woman on the beach had thrown a ball with one of those bendy launchers. Jonah watched a black dog race across the wet sand after it. The Tate appeared then hid with each rise and fall of the gentle swell. The little white graves on the cemetery hill waved back at him, and there the bowls club, Victorian villas, council houses, the row of changing cabins like bad teeth. Each element contributed to an overarching fragmentation of ugliness that fascinated him. The bay was an auditorium of bad-tempered adults all refusing to talk to or even look at each other. It was quintessential.

Jonah looked away toward the framing horns of headland that hadn't been fucked up by councilors, planners, and developers. Just rocks, the stubby coarse grasses. Seagulls. He tried to imagine what the bay would have looked like before the asphalt and concrete had arrived. It must have been just the grass and rocks of the moors right down to the beach, like farther along the coastal path. It could have been exotic. Magical. All gone.

Jonah decided to paddle back in – there wasn't even enough swell to hitch a ride. No matter. He wasn't like the others. Taking his father's old longboard out was enough: he'd gone to communion and had reaffirmed his connection with the impermanence of the sea.

It was bright for early morning, the sun just peeping over the Mount and the beach filling up with the gray light and the night faded into the purple shadows along the base of the studios by the Digey. Jonah tied up the board and adjusted the rope sling he had made around the fins before heaving up the weight of it. The cord cut into the shoulder of his wetsuit as he stumbled a little in the sand, but he had all the energy of the cold sea in him still and that would get him up Porthmeor Hill and on to Penbeagle all right. He had an hour before school; time enough to pass through the cemetery.

Jonah stopped at the beach shower near the lifeguard's office to get the worst of the sand off the board.

"Hey, Jo!"

Jonah turned at the sudden call from above. It was Ian Weekes, the bass player from The Tonix, a rival band. But they got on okay, even shared stuff sometimes. Jonah flicked his hair, thick with sand, back out of his eyes.

"All right?"

"You going back home?"

"Yep."

"Surf's up Jo," Ian laughed.

Jonah glanced back at the flat sea before pulling up on the ropes round his board.

"Yeah, got a couple of hang-tens for sure."

There was no answer. Ian had disappeared from the edge of the wall. Jonah saw just the top of the Tate frowning down instead. He shrugged and began the steep walk up to the road.

"So, you ain't going in today?" Ian had come round the corner to join him. Jonah kept walking and the two teenagers began to saunter on along the side of the sandy street.

"Sure. I've got an art exam. You're up early," said Jonah.

"Took my gran's dog out. Bit of money ain't it?"

"Oh right, sure."

"Heard you guys got a gig at the Acorn."

Jonah glanced behind for traffic before he began to cross over to the cemetery side. He nodded.

"Yep. You coming?"

"When is it?"

"Weekend. Saturday."

There was a pause. Jonah ignored it.

"Simon still mad at you?" came Ian's voice from slightly behind. Jonah pushed through the gate into the cemetery and glanced back.

"Mad at me? Er, no. What you on about?"

Ian's eyes narrowed mischievously. He shrugged.

"Nothing. Just heard."

"Heard what?" Jonah turned and began walking on. He hadn't wanted company like this. He had hoped to head back on his own.

"Just you being late and stuff."

Jonah shook his head and laughed.

"And stuff. Whatever."

There was an awkward silence as the two carried on up the steps toward the first graves and the grass.

"So, what happened to your Nan's dog?"

"Nothing. Gave it back."

Jonah wasn't listening. He'd started up the steep bank that led to the small chapel. He had been unsettled by Ian's news. It was news to him, for sure. It was all he needed.

Jonah beetled on. He was a bit annoyed that Ian was hanging by like this. He wasn't particularly a friend. He wasn't particularly friendly, either. Bit of a twat, to be honest.

"So, you got anything lined up?" Jonah decided to ask. He wasn't interested. Just making polite conversation. Changing the subject too.

"Battle of the Bands is coming up, isn't it?"

Jonah could hear Ian's labored breathing behind. He smiled to himself.

"Sure."

"That your dad's old board?" Ian puffed suddenly.

It was an unexpected and dangerous change of subject. Jonah tensed but shrugged it off. He didn't want to answer. He didn't like being provoked and now he seemed to have gotten stuck with the guy. Shit on the shoe.

Ian must have seen he'd touched a nerve. He was sensitive or decent enough not to push it.

They walked on around the small chapel. The front was covered in graffiti tags and there were empty cigarette packets and pellets of dog muck on the path close by.

"So, you headed back home at all?" asked Jonah. He wasn't sure where Ian lived. Alexander Terrace, maybe. They'd part company at the road above the cemetery in that case. But he still wanted to see the grave. He wouldn't be able to get rid of him before then. It was too bad. Jonah sighed to himself.

"There's a fox what lives here. You know that? It's crazy. I've seen it."

Jonah hadn't seen the fox. His companion was full of news. It interested him.

"Really?"

Ian had stopped to get his breath back. They were on the terrace of tombs that Jonah wanted to see.

"Yes. Just up there. It's like a demented dog. Runs round, like. I mean, like it wants to come up to you but it goes mental. Round in circles." Ian paused before going on. "They can bite, you know. Council should sort it out."

Jonah nodded.

"Maybe."

He moved the heavy board and readjusted the cords on his shoulder.

"I'm going this way. Just along here," he said.

The grave was a bit farther on. He might even be able to see it, settled there low. He didn't wait for a reply but moved away.

"What is it?" asked Ian trailing along behind.

"Alfred Wallis."

"Who?"

Jonah shook his head and laughed.

"Alfred Wallis. His grave's just there. Don't you know anything?"

"Who's Alfred Wallis? You know him?"

"Here. It's just here," said Jonah. He removed the board and let it rest against a grave. It was good to get the weight off his arm.

"That it? What's that then?" asked Ian, stepping alongside. The two looked down on the brown tiled tomb. It looked a little like a kitchen sideboard.

"Those are Leach's tiles."

"Who?"

Jonah glanced at his intrusive companion.

"Bernard Leach. He was a world famous ceramicist. And this is Alfred Wallis's grave. A humble grave."

"Whatever."

Jonah frowned.

"People have made a lot of money out of this guy. He died a pauper and they dumped him here."

"What's the lighthouse on there?"

"That?" Jonah shrugged. "Alfred Wallis was the ancient mariner. An artist."

"Oh. Right. So you came here before?"

Jonah nodded. He reached for the ropes and glanced down before lifting up the surfboard.

"I need to get going. I'll be late for school," he said, turning away.

"Sure. You're definitely going to be late. Can't go to school in a wetsuit. You're always fucking late."

• • •

Elise had gone to Truro. Hugh had taken himself a little into hiding and now sat in the bedsit Elise had made up for him in Jack's studio. There were specks of rain beginning to flick against the window. He could see the limit of the pale slate sea beyond the roof of the main house, and the bulging darker grays and sulking mauves of a sky already wintry, with its tumbling black crows and silver gulls blown sideways along the top of the junipers, then out of sight. It was nearly the end of British summertime with the last weekend of the month coming up. Mankind played with the passage of time. Chopping, cutting, redirecting it so that the smooth flowing dimension clicked and ticked mechanically forward and occasionally back. Jack was supposed to be calling later in the evening. It would be good to see him for a quick chat maybe, after Elise and the children.

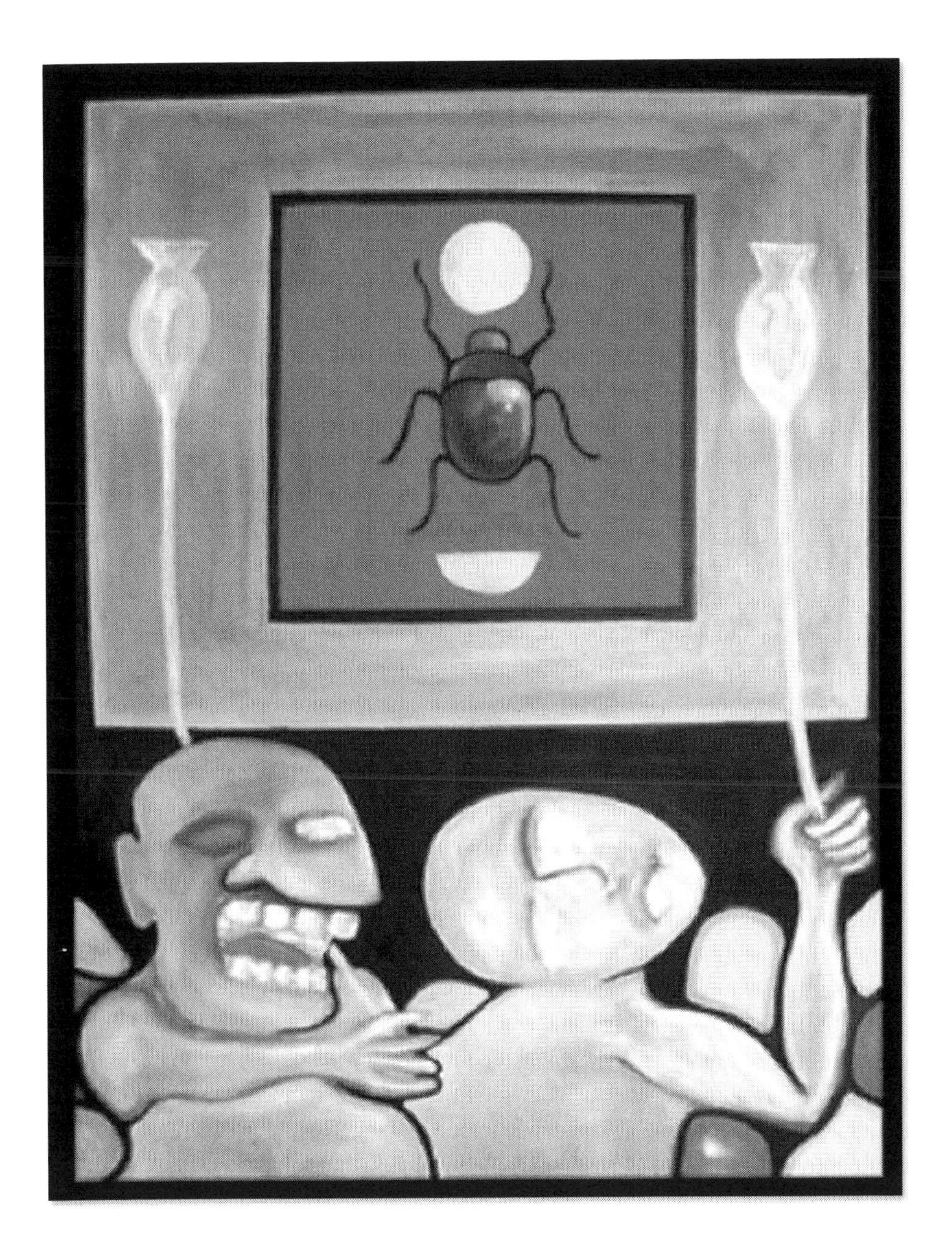

BEETLE WITH IMBECILES
CLOVIS HENRI GAUGUIN

NOVEMBER

6

"That you, Jonah?"

Jonah removed his shoulder from the front door. He had tried to slip in without his mum hearing. What was she doing up so early anyway? He could hear her in the kitchen. Banging down a mug. A drawer slammed. A teaspoon dropped and a curse. It was enough to have him looking to the stairs. He'd skip grabbing something to eat before heading back out to school. He was late, anyway.

"Just going," he called down the passage.

A shadow moved and there was no answer. Jonah pushed away from the door and darted up the narrow staircase, pulling at the back zipper tag on his wetsuit as he went. It was leaving a watery trail behind him up the tatty carpet and floorboards. With any luck, he'd be washed, changed into his school uniform, and out the door again before she emerged from the kitchen. Jonah slipped into his narrow bedroom.

He had come to know when she would be all fogged up and lost. It was almost instinctive. There were rhythms and cycles imprinted in his mind like tide tables. How out of it she would be depended on when benefit came through. Days of the week were less important. Times of the day were the most regular. Jonah leaned forward and rolled the legs down on his wetsuit. He pulled at the ends to release his feet. They were blue and numb from the cold. She was, in fact, up unusually early. He hadn't expected her to be around.

He frowned at the consideration but there were more important and immediate concerns whizzing through his mind. Ian Weekes had really bugged him. He couldn't get that out of his head. Not since leaving the beach. And his art exam. Christ! The day was already piling up. It had been fine until fucking Ian Weekes. It was as if he had sought him out deliberately just to have a go at him.

Jonah grabbed his school shirt off the back of a chair. It was crumpled. Embarrassing. So, what would the guys be cooking up? What was waiting for him to screw up his day as soon as he arrived for homeroom, which he'd now miss? He knew Simon was off him lately. Snarky comments.

Shit.

"Where's my bloody tie?"

Jonah scrabbled round, glancing this way and that. He'd lost his tie. It was getting hard to grab at any sense of priority. Everything mattered and nothing was important: the mantra of suburbia and the small town.

• • •

Jack Rockshaw watched for a gap in the traffic and stepped off the sidewalk. He had arranged to meet Amy before she had dashed off from the apartment a few hours back. Manhattan still felt like an unfinished painting. Bits sketched in to be completed maybe later or rubbed out and started again. He had walked over from the Broadway–Lafayette subway and west toward what he hoped was Sixth Avenue. He still found New York's grid system confusing and, as he wandered apprehensively down West Houston Street, he felt he was heading to the Lower Eastside. Amy had given him careful and strict instructions. She had left him early for morning class and he didn't have a map. Instead, she had written down some street names on a torn piece of cream cartridge paper. She'd meet him at a bar on Spring Street after heading over from NYU. Why didn't he just take the subway? Why did the English always have to walk everywhere? She had questioned him like his daughter: half-mocking, half-respectful.

He had walked sufficiently far for him to feel the need to remove the instruction list in his pocket. He unfolded it and glanced down: Left

King's Street to Sixth Ave. His mind was more on the handwriting than the information it conveyed. The curves and lines were bold, and though rushed, they looked unhurried. They spoke off the page with Amy's dusty voice. He felt great all of a sudden and he lowered the paper without a care.

Amy had wanted him to see a small gallery on Vandam Street. It had come out of their conversation during the night. Distractedly, he had gabbled on about nocturnal states of being and seeking out the dark places. His own end of semester exhibition was called *Obfuscation*. Amy loved his work: chiaroscuro and soft focus. Trying to blur the divide between photography and painting. Still.

"So, does 'fuscation' mean like fusion?" she had asked. The conversation was picked up by her over a hurried, standing, bedroom breakfast: bagel in one hand and mug of strong black coffee in the other. She was hunting around the bed, looking for her T-shirt. She stuck the bagel in her mouth and picked up one of his shirts off the floor near the sideboard. Jack watched her with fascination. He shook his head almost to shake her out of it.

"No. It means brown. Dark brown. From the Latin 'fuscus'. It's related to the word 'dusk'."

Amy removed the bagel and shook her free arm down into the sleeve of his shirt.

"Really? Wow. How about that?" She smiled with childlike excitement.

"You're going to wear my shirt?"

"Sure. You mind?" She held out her hands and looked down. The cuffs were well below the ends of her fingers.

"It's a bit big." She looked up. "Obscure? Is that related?"

Jack sat himself up. He felt exhausted.

"Um. I'm not sure. The 'ob' bit is, I suppose. It means to get in the way of. But I don't think 'scure' is connected to 'fuscare'. But don't quote me. I could be wrong."

Amy looked at him with curiosity. He could see she was turning the information around in her mind. Assimilating it. She nodded.

"Sure. Hey, I need to get going. I'm going to miss class. Shit."

She sort of stumbled back into action and dressing.

Before she left, she went over and kissed him.

"Weinstrom gallery. Vandam Street. Okay? If I don't get to the Ear Inn first for lunch." She winced. "Sorry Jack. I got to go."

A yellow cab had slowed down at the curb right by him standing there.

"Hey! Mister, mind out the way!"

Jack was on another planet.

"What?"

The car jerked to a stop.

"Gonna get yourself killed. Jeez. Hell, you need a cab or you just jaywalking?"

Jack waved apologetically and brought himself back into focus. He shook his head.

"No, no. Sorry."

The cab driver seemed distant, down in the gut of his yellow car. There was a pause before more words drifted up. They sounded strangely gentle. More concerned.

"You ain't lost. Need a cab?"

Jack felt himself sliding into a conversation with a complete stranger he didn't want right now. Not ever, really. He waved his hand and tried to smile. He didn't want to speak – add a line to some dialogue that had to go nowhere. Might even be dangerous. He felt his English reserve come racing to the rescue.

"No. I'm fine."

"You British?"

"Thanks. I'm fine."

Jack began to step away from the curb and he turned to walk on. He felt a rising anxiety. Don't fucking stand on street corners staring into space.

"Okay, man. Well, you have a nice day."

Jack glanced around. He was already automatically walking away. He managed to wave and smile back thankfully. From the corner of his eye, he saw the big yellow car pull out and start to slip into the traffic.

Jack strode on with more purpose and made sure he didn't drift off. That had been one of his out-of-frame experiences. He had quite enjoyed it, the sensation of things being offset, incongruous, vague, and undefined. He glanced back, before turning into King Street, and he put his hand down into his trouser pocket to adjust himself.

• • •

"Hugh? Oh, there you are. You okay?"

The door to Jack's side studio – and now Hugh's temporary abode – had been left open. Elise peered in. The stone had arrived while she had been down to the gallery in St. Ives for the morning. Hugh was just coming out from the bathroom. He hadn't heard her. Elise smiled in.

"Oh sorry. Stone looks great. It arrived then."

Hugh peered at her. He seemed a little distant as he came to the door. He nodded, then smiled.

"Can I look?" asked Elise, stepping away from the door.

"Sure. How was your morning?"

"Oh fine. Actually, I was on the phone with the quarry. You know. They can be buggers, I tell you. It's all boring but they brought it. It's so exciting. You excited?"

Elise waited for Hugh to emerge into the damp November afternoon to join her.

Hugh shrugged and came up closer. She felt a suppressed energy in him and it pleased her but she was careful not to say anything.

"Well, it feels good. I mean, to touch it. The weight of it. They were careful with the floor. I was a bit worried. They've put in a wooden plinth to spread the weight."

Elise nodded and couldn't help herself. She put her arm through Hugh's and tugged him toward her.

"Come on. I want you to show me. I want to take a photo. Well, maybe later. Come on."

She led him around the front of the barn. They reached the door and she released Hugh's arm to lift the latch. The door swung open and Elise stepped in. She glanced around. Hugh's silhouette filled the doorway.

"It's bigger than I imagined. Oh wow, it's beautiful!"

She moved forward, drawn by its thick raw gravity. She sensed Hugh stepping up close behind her. The granite was a deep gray and evenly flecked with white quartz. The wide space of the studio and the brown woods of the floor and exposed roof beams redefined the rock as it sat, exuding a brooding intimidation there on its rough timber stage. They had entered the cage of a wild animal still asleep. Hugh passed her and went up to the stone. It was almost five feet tall and a foot and half wide – up to Hugh's collarbone. She watched Hugh reach out and he seemed to stroke the front of the stone with the tips of his fingers. She felt him transported and watched him intently as he continued around the sides and the back of the megalith. She wanted to join him but didn't dare. Hugh reappeared and faced her. He grinned.

"Must be about two tons."

"Oh, Hugh. You don't need inspiration from anywhere else. All you needed has arrived."

Hugh half-nodded in agreement then glanced at the granite mass and turned to face it. There was a moment's silence before he answered.

"It's good clean stone, Elise. Hard as iron." He reached out again, unable to keep his hands off it. "Iron. Silent, hard iron. God!" He looked back at Elise, his fingertips still caressing the gritty surface of the block. "One of us will die this winter."

Elise frowned and then shook her head.

"No. It will be an exchange."

Hugh turned down the corners of his mouth thoughtfully before nodding a little.

"Yes. I forget these things."

He raised his hands and examined his fingers. He rubbed the palm of one hand with the thumb of the other. He turned to Elise.

"Look. Know this? Skin and bone. One knock and I bleed like a ripe apricot." He raised his hand to his temple and tapped the side of his head with his forefinger. "We'll see how it goes. See how it goes."

"Well, I don't know about you, but I'm going to celebrate. *We're* going to celebrate. Come on. Before Simon and Caja get back from town. Let's open a bottle of something. You coming?"

Hugh shook himself and came over to join her as she turned for the door.

"Yes, okay. I need to unwind."

Elise laughed as she stepped back out into the gathering gloom. The clocks had been set back last week and she was still getting used to the change in the light – everything now shadowed as though the days had become old.

"Oh Hugh, cheer up. Let yourself go. Seize these moments for what they are."

"No. Sure. I'm fine. I mean, I'm happy."

Elise looked at him as he came out behind her, closing the door. She wasn't satisfied.

"Not fine. You're great. Aren't you? Really. You must feel, well, elation. Joy."

They began to walk back to the house side by side.

"I feel all the intensity. You know, like I have always done. But things have changed. It's different this time. But it's good. I think. It's good to change. Mature."

Elise nodded.

"Of course. Even the rock will change."

Hugh nodded.

"Yes. But this time I feel sad. I will change things but they're perfect as they are. Human creativity has a sort of destructiveness about it. We don't make things. We just impose ourselves."

Elise shrugged. She wanted wine and lightness and laughter.

"Well. I don't know. Let's relax. Let's talk and have fun. Can't we?"

Hugh nodded.

Okay. Sure. I'll lighten up. Elise?"

"What?"

"I hope Jack calls tonight."

Elise slowed. A frown hovered.

"Of course. I'm sure he'll manage to get through. They've been having bad weather all this week."

7

"What'ya think?"

Jack's mind skipped through a chain of diffractions before he could answer: from the photograph on the wall, Amy's strawberry blond hair, her sandy voice, and then back to the picture. He realized he could see over the crown of her head. His eyes had been held fast by the nape of her neck just visible above the collar of his crumpled white shirt, slouched around her. He glanced over her right shoulder at the black and white photograph of half the side of a naked man, a leg, elbow, buttock, ankle. Right on the edge of the frame. The rest of the picture was empty space. The idea was repeated in the work along the wall in front of them, down to the end of the gallery.

Jack stepped from behind her and came alongside.

"Okay. Let's talk about it. Not here. A café?"

Amy smiled while keeping her eye on the picture before them.

"Sure. You sound bored. Everyone's talking. No one listens." She looked at him suddenly. Jack felt she was searching. He put his arm round her shoulders. She leaned into him.

"No. Not bored. I'm feeling critical and analytical and," he relaxed his arm to look at her, "there's nothing worse than seeing people in galleries talking about art and what they think they're seeing. Sorry."

Amy unfolded herself out of his arm.

"But it's what you were talking about last night." She was frowning at him.

Jack glanced at the wall. He nodded and sought to smile away any offense.

"I love it. I mean. I love that you did this. Brought me here. See? Creative works are nodes. You know, you're a butterfly. Everything that draws you is a flower."

"Well, that's cute. The frame, Jack. The frame thing. It's here. Sara Choixu had your idea."

"You think so?"

"Sure. She got to the wall before you that's all."

"Maybe."

"Bar?"

Amy reached out and tugged his belt. He felt the tips of her fingers squirrel a little down.

"You mad at me being late?"

"Of course not."

She released him and began to turn away.

"Well. There's something else I learned today. Let's get wine. How about Volare? It's kind of tucked away on Fourth and Sixth. It's not far."

"Is there a band?"

Amy laughed.

"Don't worry. No band. I promise."

• • •

"No. Michael's old enough, Hugh. Maybe he's not online yet. It's only been, what –"

"Nearly two weeks."

"Two weeks. There. It's no time."

Elise raised the second bottle of wine she had just opened. Hugh pushed his glass toward her across the kitchen table. He sighed and leaned back a little.

"It's my own fault. I'm being stonewalled. Really. He won't write back. I know he won't. And then it'll just get harder and harder as time goes on. And that's it. All gone."

"No. Hugh. Give yourself a break."

Hugh glowered back. He shook his head and crossed his arms.

Maybe the wine hadn't been such a good idea. She poured but didn't push his glass back.

"Well? You came here to get away from it all. The stone's here. I don't know. I mean, turn this whole thing into something positive. The best creations rise from ashes."

"Gone, Elise." Hugh leaned heavily forward, elbows on the tabletop at her. "Come on, let's face it, teenagers are fucking hard to connect with at the best of times. They only ever need some pathetic excuse to hate you."

Elise was careful not to respond. She could see the wine was taking Hugh around to the back of a bad place. She sighed and gave a slight shrug.

"Okay. Sure. I just want you to get into creating something. You have to use this somehow. It's what you do. It's why you do this. You've always channeled yourself."

"And *her*. Don't forget her."

Elise felt intrigued suddenly. She leaned toward him smoldering there.

"So, okay. Suppose you hadn't married Marianne but some gorgeous, loving sweet thing. Like me. A loving marriage. A dream not a nightmare. You think you would have produced such great work? I mean, Hugh, your work is wonderful. People love it. It speaks to them. You know?"

Hugh seemed to relax a little at the deliberate compliments. His face softened.

"That's just suppose stuff, Elise. What if? If things had been different, they would have been different. That's all."

"That's not what I'm saying, Hugh. I'm saying that out of negatives come positives. I'm actually referring to facts."

Hugh nodded slowly to himself.

There was the bang of a door closing from the front hall. It caught their attention and they both looked to the sound. Elise began to rise automatically.

"Must be the kids." She glanced up at the kitchen clock on the wall above Hugh's head. "They're back early."

Hugh sighed. Elise looked at him and bit her lip.

"Okay. Well, we'll talk more later. Your wine's there."

Before she could say anything else, Simon appeared at the kitchen door from the front hall. He glanced at Hugh and raised his hand a little tentatively in greeting.

"Hi."

Hugh turned, smiled, and leaned back.

"Hi Simon."

"No Caja?" asked Elise. She was returning to the table and Hugh.

"Er. No. She's in town with Jessica. Blimey, I'm starving. Anything to eat?"

Simon had already moved over to the fridge in the far corner and was opening the door; looking inside for something. He continued to speak as he rummaged. Elise sat down and the two adults watched the temporary invasion.

"Oh, um, can we have band practice tomorrow? Cheese. Cool. I mean, any chance of the guys coming over?"

Simon rose, a block of cheddar in one hand and a jar of pickles in the other. He pushed the fridge door shut with his foot and looked back to his mother.

"Simon, we talked about this." She looked at Hugh.

There was a moment's awkward silence. Hugh shook his head and raised his hand.

"It's fine. Don't worry. Really."

"No, Hugh. We all talked about this before you came. Didn't we Simon?"

Her son looked at Hugh almost as if he'd already found a key ally.

"Um. Sure. But." He shrugged and frowned, turning to put the cheese and pickles down on the side counter behind him. "It's just –"

"Push, push, push. Simon."

Hugh stepped in.

"Really. It's fine. Look, I'm not doing anything tomorrow. I was going for a walk. I wanted to go along the coastal path. How long's it take to get to St. Ives?"

Elise looked as if she wanted to continue the protest. Hugh was definitely not helping.

Simon was quick to answer.

"Oh yeah. It's a great walk. You'll see loads of seals this time of year. Specially near the Carracks." He turned back to his cheese and started to get some bread out. He spoke more assuredly. "It'll probably take you about four hours. Bit longer if you stop off for a bite. You know. Take some sandwiches. Flask. We went in the summer. Me and Jonah. Remember, Mum? That bloke with the twisted ankle. They had to get a helicopter in the end. The guy was really embarrassed."

Elise watched her son. He was so like Jack. Willful and smart. Quick to take an opportunity. She was annoyed but oddly reassured. Secretly pleased.

"Hugh, what time did you want to head off?" She wanted to re-establish some sense of control over these two.

Hugh raised his eyebrows. He shrugged.

"Well, I don't know. Maybe mid-morning. You got anything planned?"

"Hey mum, why don't you go too? Mr. Davies is bringing the gear over. That reminds me, I better text Jonah."

"Simon Rockshaw, you're a smooth operator!" Elise was annoyed. Her son was cutting his sandwich in two.

"What?"

Elise looked at Hugh and shook her head.

"Were *we* like this at that age? You know, I'd never be so, so –"

"Cocky?" offered Simon.

"Yes. Absolutely. Cocksure." She sighed theatrically and not without a little good humor. She wasn't a poor loser, at least not when her son got the better of her.

Hugh glanced down at his watch. He leaned forward a little.

"Well, in any case, you know I can't do anything until my tools arrive. Hopefully next week. Actually, well, are you free tomorrow? Fancy a blast of Atlantic air?"

Elise looked at her wineglass. The alcohol had relaxed her. In spite of a distant anxiety about Jack not calling last night, she felt content enough. Tomorrow was Sunday. She wanted to help Hugh if she could. Mother him a little. She began to nod half at the idea.

"Well, okay. Are you sure? Don't you want some solitude?"

Hugh shook his head.

"No. Not yet. In time, I might."

• • •

"*Owl in Flight*. 1988."

"You went to the Sven Berlin exhibition? *The Dark Monarch*?"

"Yes. Of course. Here. These are notes on his drawings in *Amergin*. I think it was his last novel. Did you read it, Miss?"

"No. But I've got his collected letters to John Paddy Browne. You might be interested. They were written during the *Dark Monarch* libel case. Some good stuff on the importance of the unconscious. I'll bring it into school on Monday if you like."

"Thanks, Miss. Yes. I'd love to see that. There's not much in the library at all. It's strange."

Mrs. Jerwood leaned back from looking over Jonah's shoulder.

"Maybe. But they turned his studio into a public toilet. You know that. Terrible, really."

Jonah closed his class sketchbook and nodded.

"Yes. It haunts me when I go past – sort of funny tragic. Don't like Porthgwidden for that. The others were pretty bad to him."

"Who?"

"The others. You know, Nicholson, Hepworth. He was too honest."

"It's complicated. But anyway, he produced some of his best work after leaving. Certainly his sculptures improved. Not so sure about his painting. Those psychedelic colors."

"Sure."

"Okay, Jonah. It's time to go home. You've got a great sketchbook already. And your coursework is really coming along. How's your mum?"

Mrs. Jerwood stepped back as Jonah pushed his chair to stand. She clocked his hesitation halfway on getting up.

"She's fine."

Jonah cleared his throat. There was a moment's silence.

"Look, you have a good weekend, Jonah."

"Thanks, Miss. Thanks. Got band practice at Simon's place on Sunday." Jonah turned and smiled. "Oh, and guess what?"

Mrs. Jerwood started moving to the door. She pushed a chair back under a table.

"What's that?" She looked at him.

"You know Hugh Borne, the sculptor?"

"Yes. Of course."

"Well, he's down for the winter at the Rockshaw's place. He's working on a piece in the barn."

Mrs. Jerwood was impressed.

"Wow. Simon's father away?"

Jonah nodded.

"Left for New York last week."

"It would be wonderful if you could meet him. I'm sure Simon's mother will introduce you. How exciting."

Jonah looked down at his shoes.

"Okay. Well I'd better get going. Have a good weekend Mrs. Jerwood."

"You too, Jonah. Take care."

8

Jack followed Amy down the basement steps of Volare.

"Do they do lunch?"

Amy looked back.

"Sure. Relax. You're so British."

"I *am* British. Cornish, actually. It's two already."

"They're really friendly. We can have a drink. It's the sort of place they'll let you yaddega-yadda all day. All night. I know how much you like to talk. Just kidding."

Amy pushed the door at the bottom. They were in some kind of basement restaurant. It looked lighter and less rundown than Jack had expected. Just a restaurant with no live music wires and amps stacked up against raw brick walls. He felt almost guilty.

A waitress came up, took their coats, and found them a table before heading off for a drink menu.

"See?" Amy began to sit. "Intimate. Quiet. Friendly. No strings and definitely a place for lovers."

Jack smiled back.

"Okay, good choice. So, what's this theory of yours?"

Amy adjusted herself opposite. Then she looked firmly into Jack's eyes.

"Well, it's not a theory really. Just something I picked up in cognitive psych class. I thought it might interest you. Actually, I'm more interested to see how you'll spin it."

"So, what is it?"

The waitress returned for their drink order.

Jack frowned a little and glanced at Amy.

"Why don't we just get a bottle of something and some nibbles?"

Amy looked at the waitress.

"Sounds good to me. Okay."

"You do snacks?"

The waitress nodded.

"Sure. How about blinis? Smoked salmon, we can do that for you."

"Sounds perfect. And a good house white. Italian."

"Pinot Grigio?"

Jack glanced at Amy. She nodded back. The waitress smiled and left them.

"Theory."

"Right. Well, hmm, it's complicated. I mean, I had it straight this morning in class but now it's not so easy to explain. Okay, we're doing stuff on working memory and attention. You know different effects, like the Stroop effect, and cognitive models like James's spotlight and more recent stuff, like Baddeley, um, the executive function and control over the visual spatial sketchpad? And –"

"Okay. I'm lost."

Amy bit her lip with frustration.

"Darn!"

"Start again. Why's this going to interest me?"

Amy's eyes lit up.

"Sure. Okay, what you were saying last night. You know, about wanting to sort of exist outside the day. It kind of made me think of James's idea of attention having a spotlight and a sort of vaguer and vaguer fringe moving out to a horizon. You know there's a whole lot of research these days on attention and focus and working memory and how we select what we want to see. I just thought about what you were saying and somehow I guessed these models about individual brains can be models for all society and culture, right?"

"Okay," replied Jack hesitantly. He had caught the waitress in the corner of his eye; she was bringing their wine over.

Amy saw Jack's attention had wandered. She leaned forward intensely.

"Jack. Listen to me. This is important."

"I'm listening. I'm listening. It sounds fascinating."

The waitress had reached their table. Amy began to pout.

"There you go. Pinot Grigio. And I'll just open this here and let you taste."

Jack saw Amy was restless. Intense.

"Actually, no, no. It'll be fine, I'm sure. You can just pour. Thanks," he said.

"Okay sir."

"Fact is, Jack, you just can't divide your attention. You don't get the practice. In New York, we have a gazillion things going on at once. We're made to multitask. We can listen to live music, talk, eat pizza, send a voicemail, all at the same time and it doesn't freak us out."

The waitress was pouring the wine into their glasses. Half-listening.

"And anyway, you're a man. Whatd'ya know about multitasking? Jack. You. English male. One degree of visual angle."

Jack began to laugh.

"What's that supposed to mean?"

"Put your index finger up out in front like this." Amy raised her arm in front of her across the table at him. Jack smiled and mimicked her.

"Okay."

"See your fingernail?"

"I see it."

"That's the degree of your life's focus."

The waitress chuckled.

"Sorry sir. I'll go get your blinis."

Jack lowered his arm.

"Normal people, it's a minimum. You, it's the max."

"You're saying I'm narrow-minded?"

"Kind of." Amy smiled and looked at her glass. "Hey. Bottoms up old boy."

"Whoa, whoa. What *are* you saying? I might be interested."

Amy was already sipping her wine. There was a bloom of condensation around the glass. She shrugged.

"I've no freaking idea. I guess I lost it."

"Really?"

Amy nodded. There was that naughtiness in her blue eyes. Jack was momentarily transfixed and she knew it. She loved it.

"No. You had something there. The bit about culture. Society."

"Really?"

"Oh come on, Amy. You're playing games with me. Actually, it's very sexy. I love it. Tell me more. Make sense before I get drunk." Jack leaned away from her against his chair. "Sometimes we sort of tread on stars. We grasp stars almost without realizing. Then they slip. Gone. The stars come about halfway through the second bottle of wine. Amy, we still have time. Tell me. I'm listening. I have all of my one percent attention on you."

Amy laughed.

"One degree, Jack. See, I knew you weren't listening."

"Well, if you're so smart, young lady, how come I can't focus on what you're saying even though I've got such laser-beam ability?"

"Disability."

"God I'm glad you're not in my photography class."

"Well, actually, what you haven't got is a wide-angle."

"I haven't got a wide-angle."

"That's right. But it's not important. It's not connected so much with what I wanted to say. I mean, what matters is what you choose to put in the frame. Portrait or landscape doesn't matter. It's what is put in. You see? Sara Choixu."

Jack began to see something. He nodded slowly.

"Okay. Okay, I got the end bit, maybe. Figures on the margin. Sara Choixu. By the way, is that her real name, you think?"

Amy smiled.

"Of course not. They're all made up. It's a marketing thing." She leaned forward conspiratorially. "Look, the City's just a huge gut we call Fifth Avenue. The mouth is Washington Square and its ass is Central Park. See?"

"Arse."

"Ass. To get from one end to the other, you need to get noticed, the right gallery, the right people, the right marketing, reviews, blah blah yadda schmuckadda, and the right name. Helps if it's unpronounceable like with no vowels in it. Get the right combination and your work moves smoothly along the canal. If there was anything authentic at the point of ingestion, that's leached out when it gets to the other end, by which time they've turned it into shit. Expensive shit."

Amy looked down.

"You sound angry."

"You mean mad? Sure. I'm mad. The ass end is killing the truth end. No one decent can live here. It's too expensive. The good guys have been banished upstate. The edges."

Jack nodded.

"That's where creativity belongs. Perhaps the visual angles just keep getting bigger?"

Amy looked up and the sun came back out.

"See? You got it."

• • •

Hugh propped up his iPad on the little desk beneath the windowsill. Jack's study room was dark save for a pool of light from the standard lamp near the sofa bed behind him. He had put the heater on but the air was chill. Damp. His mind flicked to the studio next door and how it would be so cold in the coming winter months. He felt the spirit of the stone proud and resilient still. His *Mordwand.* He had begun to feel himself on the edge of his vision: the merciless cold, his breath like blue smoke suspended, the insistent dark and the shallow days and the long shadows, the pain in his swollen hands. The blood and his blue knuckles. Hugh turned his eyes on the iPad. He pressed the screen and swiped for Jack's last iMessage.

• • •

Jack touched his screen. Hugh was calling him. He leaned back carefully and waited for the connection to come through. He felt prepared well enough for this.

"Hugh. Hi. Thanks for getting back. Just thought it'd be easier to catch up on stuff. You know. You okay?"

The face in the picture hadn't quite clocked him. The light from behind distorted the contours.

"Hi Jack? You there?" The eyes peered blindly.

"I'm here. Can you see me?"

"Hang on. Something's wrong. Oh. There you are." The face smiled. A hand moved away into the enfolding darkness. "Thought I'd lost you."

Jack smiled. Hugh looked tired. He'd aged.

"There've been some late season storms. Maybe it's a poor signal."

The head nodded.

"Maybe. But the signal's not so good here either. Stormy weather, hey Jack?"

Hugh's voice sounded distant. Some words were breaking up. They weren't going to get a decent conversation going. Jack tensed.

"Sure. So, um, the stone arrived. That's great. You in the vibe?"

Hugh seemed to look away. The head nodded tentatively.

"I'll get there. Tools should arrive next week. I want to keep the cutters down to a minimum. I'm bringing the Italian chisels. I'm excited about them. Cost a bloody fortune."

"Cool. Don't be hard on yourself, Hugh. You okay?"

The head nodded and the eyes were back searching.

"I'm fine, Jack. How's New York?"

"Oh, the students are okay. Really. But not much going on. Know what I mean?"

Hugh smiled.

"You're picking up the accent there Jack."

Jack laughed.

"They all think I'm a pirate."

"You are. Wish I could be there."

"Well, we're both in the colonies, I guess. Just hanging off the back pockets of the world always too busy to look around. So much good stuff here. Just trashed. Lost. What are we doing, Hugh?"

"I don't know."

"Why don't you come over for Christmas?"

Hugh looked puzzled.

"Whatd'ya mean? I thought you were back here for the break."

"I am. I was thinking you might like a break yourself. I'm keeping the apartment. It'll be empty. Why not use it?"

The face frowned – the eyes suddenly a little lost.

"Just a crazy idea."

"No, no. It's a good idea. And thanks. It's just there's so much going on, Jack. You know. And Christmas this year . . ." Hugh trailed off.

"Of course. Sure, well, leave it. You've just arrived. Sorry."

Hugh's face looked up and smiled.

"You know, I really want to get going on this project. I'm beginning to feel it. Elise is taking me along the coast path tomorrow. To St. Ives." Hugh stopped and peered. "What's that?"

Something seemed to have caught Hugh's attention. Jack glanced behind him. There was his bedroom. A chair. A table.

"What's what?"

"*That.*" Hugh was pointing.

Jack looked again and saw Amy's missing T-shirt. It was hanging off the corner of the dresser. Caught in the act and suspended in time.

Jack knew Hugh was aware he'd seen it too. Just then. His mind raced for something quick and defusing.

"Oh, the dresser? The shirt." Jack turned back and laughed gently then chuckled as if he was getting the joke of it. "It's Amy's. She must have left it here."

"Oh. I see."

Jack looked at his old friend knowingly.

"Work, Hugh. I need to add a few shots for the exhibition. She's been great. In fact, you should meet her. And I want you to see the Obfuscation exhibition. Look, give it some thought. No hassle. I just think you might want to be away from all that Christmas shit this year."

Hugh seemed a little distant. Jack was surprised at how subtle emotions still managed to come across on a crap connection. There was a sort of tired sigh in the airwaves.

9

"There! Can you see it? And there's another one. Just by the rock behind." Elise pointed. She must have seen plenty of seals over the years but she was still excited. Excited for him.

They were standing on the coastal path where it came close to the cliff edge, not so high up off the sea but elevated enough to provide a seagull's view over the little cove of pale pure sand almost glowing beneath the glass waves and separated by a midline bank of black rocks and churned, ground pebbles. The small headland to the northeast of the cove dived beneath the restless tide before rising again with a final jagged tooth that had the white foam fretting about it, busy and covetous. Hugh's eyes were on that, not hungry for seals. The rocks seemed to comb the thick locks of the sea. He was fascinated how the sides of the ocean would rise with leviathan breathing and roll off the jagged edges metamorphosed. Lifeless. Sliding back into the swell. Hugh heard the rustle of Elise's raincoat. It distracted him.

"Yes. They're wonderful. Like black Labradors," he offered a little lamely. He pulled the collars of his coat closer round his neck. There were flocks of rain in the wind. He turned and began to walk. Elise lingered a little before following.

They wandered on without talking at first. It was Elise who broke the meditation.

"Did you have a good chat with Jack? After? I'm sorry about Caja. Actually, she really misses her father. It's strange how teenagers feel they need to project the opposite. It's a shame, really."

Hugh listened. He heard a mother wanting or needing to talk about her children more than anything else. With Marianne it had bored him. But it was different with Elise. More intelligent, somehow. More willing to generalize from the personal and the particular. Not just Caja, but all adolescents.

"Michael was the same."

Elise was up close now. Hugh looked at her and she nodded but her mind was still on Caja.

"I worry," she said.

"Don't bother. There's this great gulf. And a sort of second birth. A shedding of skin like a snake. Michael will never talk to me again."

Elise now listened. Turned her mind from her daughter.

"Of course he will. One day. You don't know."

Hugh shook his head defiantly.

"I do. He's like me. Stubborn." Hugh raised his eyebrows. "Don't worry. I'm a bloke. It doesn't matter. I suppose men are more immune. Why are you worried about Caja? She seems fine to me."

"I just wish she was happier. I don't know. She was such a fun kid. I hate this, you know, transition."

"Sure. Don't worry. The anger is directed only at us. If you saw her with her friends, you'd see a different human being. Teenagers are predictable, boring, selfish shits. Fuck 'em."

Elise laughed.

"Oh Hugh. You don't mean that."

"Don't I?" He stopped. Elise almost bumped into him. The two parents looked at each other. "I'm bored, Elise. I'm bored by the sameness. God, give me a human being, just one bloody human being, who is different. Not normal. Not ordinary. A free individual in this world so proud of its free individuals. It's all so profoundly depressing. Teenagers! All exactly the same. Terrified of being different while adamant they're kooky, random, radical."

Hugh saw how much his rant was amusing Elise. He laughed back. Saw the silliness in himself exposed.

"Well, they do sort of rub off on you," she said.

"What's that supposed to mean?"

Elise shrugged.

"Nothing really. Actually, you should meet Jonah."

Elise stopped. The thought had really caught her. She looked animated. Like she'd seen another of her seals.

"Of course. Why didn't I think of that? Oh Hugh. You must meet Jonah. Jonah Singleton. And Jonah must meet you!"

Elise's face beamed sudden radiance as though she'd had a revelation.

"Jonah? Interesting name. That's at least different."

"He's in Simon's band. He's really into art. Really talented. Does the posters and the website."

"Listen. Teenagers don't really exist. That's why they're so fucked up. They're a postwar marketing invention created by toy manufacturers, the rag trade, and record companies. Coca-Cola Father Christmas."

Elise frowned.

"No, no listen. Stop ranting. In fact, exactly. You're right. But Jonah somehow missed out on being, well, being turned into a product consumer." Elise nodded to herself. "Like he was left on a desert island while his peers turned into culture clones. It's not Michael who's like you, it's Jonah." She looked down and they stopped. "Poor Jonah."

• • •

The council had sent men to stop the seagulls from nesting on the roof. They had used chicken wire but the storms had blown the netting away. The worst were the herring gulls. Big as boats when fully grown and forever tugging at the entrails of street bins. The young would appear magically on the roof: flightless, rusty gates opening and closing under the mischievous hands of boys, or gibbets swinging to and fro in the wind. The angry hungry piping was enough to drive the uninitiated and the unoccupied mind to destruction. Then the barking of the seabirds wheeling over the mackerel catches down in the harbor would rise to nail the day.

Sunday morning.

The single bell at St. Mary's began to knoll the passing of the night.

No artist had cared to portray the town gull. It was boats, harbors, the moors, fish, the fishermen's cottages in Downalong alone that filled the galleries. No gulls. In revenge, the mews had an art of their own.

Jonah waited. At ten to nine, the front door would open and the cheap house walls would then shiver with a bang. That sound was a pebble thrown into a well, the ripples pulsing out across the days of each week.

• • •

"I love it when we're naked. Don't you?"

Amy wasn't interested in a reply. She jumped at his side, knocking him hip against hip. Jack put his arm round her and yawned.

"You're going to kill me."

"Yes," she whispered loud in his ear. "Death by sex." She was in one of her electric moods. "You know, a woman could fuck a man to death if she wanted to."

"Do you want to?"

"Sure I would, if it turned you on."

Jack laughed and she felt him squeeze her, but his arm was already falling asleep.

"Oh my God, I'm still so horny. Jack. Jack don't leave me."

"I'm here."

Amy put her hand on his chest and pushed herself up. Jack grunted.

"No you're not. You're falling away."

"I'm old," he mumbled. "You need a young Italian. One of your college friends."

"Sure."

Jack opened an eye. She smiled straight in there. Her hand sliding down to play.

"Just joking. You're not *really* old. Do you like that?"

"You have a rare gift."

"Aww, Jack, I lust you so much." She squeezed gently. "Yeah, there's Renato Gambucci. He's real hot. We could fuck him." She tightened her grip

"That's a made-up name."

"It's Italian. I don't know his name. Sure. I could check him out, if you like."

She felt his hand on her back. His arm was waking.

"That turn you on?" she asked.

His hand slid down and she raised her hips for him to find her.

"That sort of thing's out of my league."

"Well, then you *are* getting old."

She felt his fingers slip into her. It still made her catch her breath.

"I'm not going to apologize for the flow of time. Yes. I'm too old, Amy. Sweet Amy."

She didn't want to talk now.

"Oh yes, just there. Don't stop."

• • •

When Jack woke the next morning, she had gone. He was still heavily drunk with sleep and the realization that Amy wasn't there tiptoed into the dormitory of his dull brain, stepping from bed to bed to shake the shoulders of other thoughts. He opened his eyes suddenly. The room was light. He must have overslept.

"Shit!"

He heaved himself up on his side and looked stupidly round the room before grasping for his watch on the bedside cabinet. Time was upside down. Turn it round. Ten past nine. God! He was going to be an hour late for class and now came all the rush of how to limit the damage. What excuse? He'd phone in sick. There was a stomach bug going round. Still getting used to the transition. Anyway, he was an artist. They had a license for such peccadilloes. Their minds were on higher things. Or maybe he just caught the wrong train. Took the 7 all the way to Flushing Meadows.

Jack was now sitting up and looking around. Why hadn't Amy woken him? The thought suddenly hit that she had left. Dumped him. No, no there was her T-shirt, still draped over the end of the dresser like a flag.

"Okay. It's all okay," he said to himself. He was going to be able to realign the vision, the picture of his life at this time. How far out did he need to reach? Beyond the bed? The bedroom. The apartment block, his contract with Hunter College, the day. The day. Or should he reach beyond the horizon to Elise? His kids? He recalled his chat with Hugh last night. Hugh had clocked it all. He had a hawk's eye and a five-hour head start on each dawn. He winced at the memory of his wriggling efforts to cover his tracks. What a dick he must have looked.

In spite of all, Jack let himself fall back, his head resting on the crumpled pillow. For the first time, he noticed the ceiling. A jagged thin line in the plaster. What would it be like if he just let it all fall apart – let all the energy spent on trying to hold it together, just go? Unlock all the valves, open up all the taps, and let everything drain away. The family, the money, the career. Everything. What he was doing now was neither here nor there. A sort of suburbia of non-commitment. Agnosticism. As he lay on the bed, Jack visualized the dash down to the Bleecker Street Subway. The heavy eyes. Rocked in the crowded car, one primate arm held up to steady himself at every stop. Thrown about in a can all the while in a fog about what he was supposed to be lecturing on. Slides. A panic for the slides. PowerPoint not working. All the day spent trying to hold it all together. Give me a silver beach, the moonlight, and a local girl riding me into oblivion. Fuck me to death.

• • •

Vases de fleurs et un éventail. Two vases of flowers. Paul Gauguin 1885 Oil on canvas Measurements 99.5 by 64cm.39 1/8 by 25 1/4 in. Signature detail: Signed P. Gauguin and dated 85 (lower center). Sold Sotheby's 25 Jun 08. Hammer price with buyer's premium: £3,513,250 GBP.

Bouquets et ceramique sur une commode. Paul Gauguin 1886 Oil Painting. Signature / Inscription details: Signed P. Gauguin and dated 86 lower left. Dimensions of painting; Height x Width: 24" x 29" (60 x 73 cm). Sold Sotheby's 19 Jun 07. Hammer Price with Buyer's Premium: £2,484,000 GBP. Housed in a Private Collection.

"Yes. 'Oh'. Can you believe it, Simon has decided to kick Jonah out."

Hugh was next to her and taking the corkscrew.

"Kick Jonah out?"

"Out of the band."

"Oh right."

Elise jabbed a wooden spoon into the chili con carne and stirred it vigorously.

"Well, it's awful."

"Is it?"

The spoon stopped.

"Yes it is. It's so cruel and unnecessary. I hate it."

She turned to Hugh for support.

"*Isn't* it?"

She saw Hugh looking at her with concern. He frowned and was serious at last.

"Yes. It is. You're crying."

• • •

There was an icy night wind blasting off the Hudson down West Fourth Street. Amy decided to head east so at least she'd have her back to it. She heard the security guys locking the doors of the Bobst Library behind her. A couple of students were just leaving. They had to open the doors again to let them out. Amy heard the voices behind. Maybe someone got locked in, like the 'Bobst Boy' – the student who moved into the library basement because he couldn't afford to live anywhere else. He had kept a sort of blog. Why did he do that? What a lameo. 'Lameo' or 'lame-o'? Like it was one big publicity stunt all along. If she was going to be the Bobst Girl, she'd just get all snug down there amongst the heating pipes. Mind her own business.

Art was a publicity stunt. Everything was about getting noticed. Why? The more the world became post-heroic, the more everyone felt the need to stand out. The world of individuality had become saturated blind with video cameras.

• • •

"Lameo is a general term that describes anyone who is completely socially retarded, does not do drugs and spends their life chasing after women and fucking with safe mateys birds. They are rediculously keen and try extremely hard at everything, especially there appearance, this is what makes them lame. A dick noone but other dicks like or hang around, the type of person you avoid and run away from and silence phone calls from and do not reply to texts . . . you know who you are you sad bastards. They are a wart on the anus of society and a drain on anyones social energy. . . they shoud be harshly ignored."

-Urban Dictionary

• • •

"Hi Mr. Rockshaw. Becky asked me to give you her assignment. Said she's sorry but can't make class today."

Jack looked up from his laptop on the desk. Other students were coming into the lecture room in dribs and drabs. Jack glanced at the young man standing in front of him: Gap jeans, Gap check shirt and hoodie, beanie, rough shaven, olive skinned. He was momentarily distracted. Looking for Amy. Maybe she would appear unexpectedly playing one of her games. He refocused and saw the essay rolled and presented like a sprinter's relay baton.

"Right. Thanks. You Becky's friend?"

"Uh, sure." The student nodded. He seemed keen to break away. Jack looked down at his laptop.

"That's two classes she's missed. One more and she's out of this elective. Maybe you could remind her of school rules."

Jack took the essay.

"Well, anyway, okay. Thanks."

The student nodded and turned to find a place to sit.

"Okay guys. Could someone close the door at the back? Thanks. Right. Yesterday we looked at some of the chiaroscuro effects used by Leibovitz and I showed you some of the lighting techniques you can adopt for outdoor digital work, portrait, and landscape. I hope some of you managed to download the Golden Hours app. It now has blue hour information. Right, today I want to look at studio lighting techniques, use of single and double key lighting and reflectors for digital work that you are not, repeat, not, ladies and gentlemen, going to fudge when shooting only to adjust later on screen. Okay? By the way, we'll be working in JPEG Raw during the workshop sessions this afternoon. I'm going to illustrate effects through some of my own work and I want you to think about how you can take the figurative into the abstract through your own explorations of light and shadow. Okay. Let's look at the first slide. Now this is obviously not a photograph. Does anyone know this painting?"

"Is it a David Jones?"

"No. Not a bad guess though. Got a Celtic feel about it. Right sort of period."

"It's *St. Just*. It's by Peter Lanyon."

Jack looked from the image on the screen. His heart leapt and all the energy began to rise through him. He had heard the dusty, obfuscated voice. But he couldn't see her.

"Good. Right. Yes. It's *St. Just* by Peter Lanyon, the Cornish artist. 1953. So, other than because this is a landscape, of sorts, from where I live, why else might I have chosen to start here?"

• • •

"Where did you go? I've been looking all over for you."

"Do you think there's a storm coming in?" Amy stopped and looked at Jack with her piercing blue eyes. "*Me*? You were looking all over New York for me?"

Jack saw she looked puzzled. It was feigned, of course. She began walking on and talked with her eyes fixed firmly ahead.

"Where are we going?" he asked.

"Well, I wasn't looking for *you* but then, suddenly there you were. It's ironic. But you know I love your work. I love hearing you talk about yourself. All *you* had to do was wait. Anyway, you weren't looking all over New York. That's just a dumb hyperbole. I don't even know what it means, but I'm figuratively flattered. Could you take me to Sarabeth's?"

"Really? It's miles."

"No it's not. Anyway, if you were searching, that's where you'd find me. Better hurry before she gets bored waiting."

Amy gave him a sideways glance.

"Aww, Jack, don't look so worried. You Brits get so uptight. I'm just playing with you."

Jack was trying to keep up with her. Where had she come from? Where was he going?

"Can't we get a cab?" he asked. At this rate, they'd hit the lunch hour rush. They'd never get a table.

She shook her head defiantly. The wind caught her hair.

"No. I love this. The winter is arriving right now. I don't want to be locked to death in a cab."

They walked on. Crossed Madison Avenue on East Sixty-Seventh.

"Why are you mad at me?"

Amy laughed.

"I'm not mad at you." She leaned toward him and took his arm.

"Then what is it?"

"What's what?"

"Why are you being all kind of – like this? Can we stop a minute?"

Jack felt her tug him closer. She put her hand up to his face and they slowed to a halt. She kissed him.

"I just want to fuck you. Do you think there's something wrong with me? Like I need to see a fuck doctor?"

Jack shook his head at her stupidly. He shrugged.

"Sure." She smiled. "It's a sort of life affirmation thing. That's all. Isn't it, Jack."

"Are you okay? Are you on something?"

"No. It's you. You're confused. I feel your disorientation like pulsing out of you. Maybe that's where the wind's coming from. Come on, I'm getting cold. You'll just have to multitask. Walk and talk like a New Yorker."

Amy let him go and carried on. Jack pushed his hands into his duffel coat pockets. They were freezing.

"You don't stop to talk. Got to keep moving. We'll cut through the park. Wow, I love this wind! Look at the leaves ripping off the trees like roof tiles in a hurricane. Wizard of Oz! Oh my god!"

Jack was alongside as they approached Fifth Avenue. Life had become a Broadway show. It was ridiculous and camp but he'd never felt so alive. So happy. So lost.

FRITZ KOENIG'S SPHERE

DECEMBER

11

Hugh circled the stone. He wanted to fast-forward his life. Drive through this month at high-speed with his eyes shut. But December had already hunkered down. Stubborn and bad tempered.

This was the third day he had come to explore the stone. It was a blank edifice. Hugh well knew that it was his hands that were the key to uniting rock and vision and, again, his fingers played over the surface of that cliff. Eyes closed. Consciousness buried somewhere far off. Under the surface, the mind stirred. Billions of connections were being made. Deep and silent. But you could feel there was movement under the surface of the sea, almost in the way the waves were distorted imperceptibly by a shoal. A paleontologist can sense a fossil buried within the clay. A geologist sees the ocean bed on a mountainside. Hugh allowed a chink of consciousness to report back that, yes, there was something. Just about. And maybe it needed a little more time, but it had begun.

Hugh opened his eyes and withdrew his fingers from the rock. He stepped back. A ripple of anxiety caught his inner eye. He had a sense that the width of the stone might not be quite great enough to capture the shoulder of the Virgin. His eyes narrowed and he stepped round deftly. Calculating. The angle of Christ would need to be just a little steeper maybe. The artist works with and within the confines of the chance materiality before him. Hugh didn't want to cut too much away. It wasn't how he crafted his work; he wasn't a miner, and his chisels preferred to gather the air, the space around the stone. Hugh felt space more than the object that filled it as if he carved and chipped into the ether itself. Perhaps it was a trick of the mind needed to prime his tendons and sinews for what was to come. That was his only real worry: broken chisel heads, and, within days, joints swollen raw and fingers too weak and stiff to hold a pencil.

The door to the barn was being opened. The sharp click of the latch startled him a little and he looked round. It was Elise.

"Can I come in? Sorry. I've disturbed you."

Hugh didn't answer at first. He had thought Elise was at the gallery. She must have come back for something. She came up. The door left open.

"Hi. All good?"

Hugh nodded.

"Hello. I thought you were in town."

"I was. Sorry. I had to come back for the storeroom keys. Such a dummy."

"You should have phoned. I could have driven them down."

"No. Not at all. Same number of trips. Anyway, look you're busy and I've disturbed you. Sorry. I'll um . . ."

Elise trailed off and began to step away. Her action of withdrawal had Hugh shaking himself.

"No. Elise. I'm just a bit spaced out. Would you like a quick coffee? I was miles away."

Elise was now at the door. She smiled back, dark against the gray light.

"No, no. You get on. I'm sorry to have interrupted. Really. Have a great morning."

"I'm coming now. I want to talk. I'm done anyway. I need a break." Hugh moved away from the wooden plinth.

Elise was already out on the path. Hugh gathered himself up and marched after her.

She was waiting. She was tense.

"What's up?" he asked. He closed the door and they walked down the path to the house together.

"Nothing."

"Yes there is."

Elise crossed her arms as she walked on. Her shoulders were a little hunched. She shook her head at him.

"No. Really. I shouldn't bring up irrelevant things. You know, when Jack's engrossed in something, well, he's not interested in hearing dull irrelevant stuff."

"Oh, right. So there *is* something. Well, try me. I'm not Jack." Hugh looked at Elise carefully. "It's about Jack isn't it?"

Elise didn't answer. They had reached the back porch to the kitchen and Elise pushed the door. The house took them in again to confine and control with all the paraphernalia of the domestic space. Another framework of conditioned responses. A dead place. Hugh felt it crawl at him.

"Coffee. Better make it quick." Elise had already switched on the kettle. She was taking mugs down from the cabinet above her head.

"You're beautiful," he said spontaneously.

Hugh had vaguely wanted to say 'lovely' or, in all truth, 'altruistic'. But it came out 'beautiful'. Perhaps the Pieta had been in his mind and he had picked out an aesthetic term rather than an ethical one by accident.

Elise glanced at him. Did she look a little startled? Would she bat back what could have come across as a come-on? Fairly inappropriately timed, at that. He knew what was worrying her, so he persisted.

"You care so much about people. You think about them all the time. You pander to egos. You sit and listen to the world when everyone else is talking and walking by. You look at art. You read books. You worry about your husband – that you'll lose him somehow."

Hugh's words were audacious enough to have Elise looking at him not with feigned surprise – maybe annoyance – but a slight nod. There were no welling tears. She looked down at the mug in her hands.

"Do I? Am I worried about Jack, do you think?"

Hugh felt she was testing him. Did he have the key? Did he see her better than she could see herself? Was she inviting him to provide a mirror?

Hugh sighed and pulled out a chair from the kitchen table. He sat down.

"Well, I do know you care so much about others. Jonah, for example. Everyone. Maybe you should be made aware of that, if you haven't already been enlightened. I'm happy to *consciousize* it for you. But Jack? Is he a worry? I mean, to you. I don't know. You tell me."

Elise turned away thoughtfully. She carried on making the coffee and seemed to prefer having her back to him for the minute.

"Well," she said, pouring the water into the French press, "you've been talking to him. Are you going to protect him?"

"Protect him?"

"Yes. I mean. Is he having an affair?"

Hugh frowned and shifted awkwardly.

"Am I supposed to know something?"

Elise poured their coffee at the side and lifted the mugs to bring them over to the table. She gave him a broken smile.

"You're fishing, Hugh."

"Am I?"

She nodded.

"Yes. The cuckold is usually the last to know. That's part of the joke and the cruelty of it, of course."

Elise's voice was calm and too level. She put their cups on the table and pulled out a chair.

Hugh cleared his throat.

"I've known Jack for years. I knew him before you met. I don't think he's the sort of guy who would have an affair." He felt Elise looking at him critically.

"Sugar's there."

"No thanks."

"And were *you* the sort of guy who would have had an affair, do you think?" she asked.

Hugh glanced back at her as he raised his coffee.

"That's a bit harsh. Look, people live in landscapes, contexts. I mean, Marianne and I –"

"It's okay. I know. I'm sorry. Do you think I'm like her?"

"No. Of course not."

"Oh. Then there are pull factors not push. I mean, in *my* situation."

"Well. Hang on. I don't know what Jack might be up to. Really."

"Really?"

Hugh nodded earnestly enough to gently hold her back.

She sighed.

"It's not the jealousy thing. It's more, I don't know, a feeling that the script has just run out. You know, you've been living on this stage acting away as if it was all real. And then the play ends before you're ready to leave. I feel rather exposed. A bit foolish standing there." She looked at Hugh and smiled. "Sitting here."

There was a silence

"I don't think –"

"And there's the children, of course."

"Elise. I don't think you need to worry. Really. Look, I'll confront him, if you like. I mean, I'll probe. Somehow. Has this happened before?"

"Has *what* happened before? My suspicion or his guilt?"

"Well, either. Both. Look, I'll speak to him tonight and I'll have a heart to heart. It's easier coming from me, don't you think?"

Elise shrugged.

"Maybe. I don't know. Oh shit. What a bore! What do I do? Hugh, you've been in this situation, what do I do? Run off to Paris? Get a divorce? Take the kids away?"

She reached out suddenly and took hold of his wrist, gently but firmly. There was such pain in her eyes.

"You see? It's difficult for us women. We have the children."

Hugh looked down. He froze.

"I know. I know."

"And then there's fucking Christmas: coming round year on year like an accusing mirror."

• • •

Jonah couldn't face school today. It was good to be on his board. The waves weren't bad, just not so regular or frequent. Two, three feet. It gave him time to gather in the morning light. There was actually a clear, bright blue sky with just a few white clouds like the first commuter cars on the morning roads. In an hour or so, they'd start stacking up sure enough. There'd be a nimbus logjam and then it would start to rain. Jonah knew the weather. West to east. The restless winds bending with the tides and angled a little offshore. The woman with the black dog had just arrived. Ball flying down the beach. Dog belting after it now, shit free and happy.

Okay, wave coming. Jonah pulled himself up the longboard. His muscles had become stiff with the cold and his limbs complained. But the sea began to lift like a horse on a giant carousel and his body ceased to exist or else melted into the rising wave. He loved his father's old board. Solid as a rock, level as a barn door. Lazy like him. He laughed at the moment of unification of wave, body, mind, and board. Paddling manically, Jonah was a neoprene black swan beating the water before launching himself into the air. The sun skimmed its first white pebbles over the Mount and they cut the bright foam and the curling sea. For less than a minute, the universe rolled through time perfectly balanced.

When you have no money, there's nothing to do. When you have nothing to do, you sit and you think. The poor are the listeners, the onlookers. The wise. But they don't know this and their innocence is their humility and their humility just makes them sit some more. And on it goes. That's what Jonah was thinking as he sat on the edge of the rocks at the end of Porthmeor beach. Thinking.

The clouds were parked up as if they couldn't get past the sun. Dumb fucking sheep blocked by a dog. The woman with the black dog had been joined by a bloke. He had a brown and white dog. Sort of half whippet, half sheepdog. Maybe? He wore a flat cap and a Barbour. Doggers. Talking about dogs and weather. And more dogs. Nothing else. Things that mattered but were unimportant. Dead words hanging out of dead minds. Dog shit.

Jonah couldn't bear them. He turned to look out along the black rocks and the headland: the bucket of the bay scooping up the waves. Some slopping out. This was heaven and this was hell. He liked that. The way the two constantly rubbed shoulders, bumped hips. And then school. He had his back facing the town world. But the great weight of it pressed down on him. He actually shifted himself to be rid of it and glanced back.

The Dark Monarch stared down on Jonah. Imperious.

12

"Amy?"

"Yeah?"

"What are you doing? I mean, what do you want to do?"

"I want to focus. I want to fuck us."

"You're being evasive. There's something really pissing you off. Why won't you tell me?"

Amy leaned back and raised her hands in front of her, both forefingers up like she was about to conduct a kiddies' mouse orchestra. Then she drew a rectangle in the air.

Jack smiled.

"Charades. Great. Film?"

"Uh-uh." She shook her head. She repeated the action, but this time the rectangle was a bit bigger.

"A painting?"

Amy lowered her hands and rested them neatly on the table. She sat still. Like a portrait.

"No. Jack?"

"What."

"I can't get out of the square of me."

"The square? What'dya mean?"

Amy sighed and looked at him. She hesitated.

"Well, like for instance, when we fuck, do you fuck me or you?"

Jack raised his eyebrows and leaned back against his chair. He nodded slowly and with understanding.

"Well," she continued. "Maybe it's brutal, but fact is, I'm doing me all the way. All the time. It's just like that. I'm sorry, I guess."

"Don't be sorry. Everyone does it like that."

"Really?"

"Maybe we graduate toward fucking *us*. I mean, like an out of body experience. I think, actually, that's where I'm at. It's not a bad thing. I mean, you'd have to be a complete doormat any other way."

Amy nodded.

"Sure. I guess. Jack?"

"Yes?"

"I'm not done. I mean, how I fuck is just a symptom. I want to get out of the ego box. Out of my body. Out. Right out there. Right out of this fucking city. Out of my head. Where the frame is so big everything is in and nothing matters. I feel it sometimes. Like when I'm floating in the middle of the Pacific, blue on blue. Like when I come."

Jack was looking round. The waitress was hovering.

"You all done?"

"Could we have more coffee? Amy? Coffee?"

Amy nodded.

The waitress smiled down and began to clear the table. The couple sat patiently. Amy chewed her lip.

"So, um, you don't get hassled at the Visitor Center – at Hunter?" he asked.

Amy shook her head.

"Coffee coming, sir."

Jack looked up.

"Thanks."

Amy was looking at him.

"Okay. So that's me. I'm not going to be able to live in this fucked up world. I'm twenty-one and I know I couldn't live even like you. You know, do all the normal stuff like bachelors, masters, hubby, babies, house, car, job, affair, divorce, um. What comes next?"

Jack was looking down but he listened as he drifted on with his own take on things. He glanced up.

"Next? Second marriage. College fees for your kids."

"Oh yeah. I forgot in advance. So, maybe a midlife crisis, breakdown, menopause, more work, pension panic, retirement, gym, watercolors, grandchildren, memory loss, death."

"You missed something."

"What?"

"Christmas."

"Oh yeah. Shoot. I forgot all the other cyclic boxes along the way."

"Amy?"

"Jack?"

"Don't disappear on me, will you?"

• • •

Hugh's tools had arrived from London. They now lay on the studio floor in three wooden cartons. It was like he was moving house. He had already opened the tops looking for the chisels. Checking for the angle grinder. Extension cables. Files. All there. Just as he had packed it before leaving the studio in Bermondsey. It had only been a couple of weeks but it felt like a reunion after a lifetime. London was another world. Hugh frowned to himself before bending down over one of the boxes. He wanted to at least unpack the tools. Check that things were all there. And it was a moving in. A sort of taking over. He felt the stone eyeing him like a patient before an operation.

He proceeded slowly. He handled each chisel, each piece of equipment with careful attention, as if to reaffirm a bond. Soon the boxes were empty and his kit now lay out on the floor beside the stone. He stepped back to assess and feel things. He wanted to spend the afternoon going through his notes. His sketches. He felt the tense excitement he knew so well and a pushing back of the clutter of life: a mental sweeping clear of a tabletop with his arm.

Hugh stepped away and turned for the barn door, still ajar. He felt the cold winter air whipping in and curling around his legs as he pulled the handle and made to leave.

But he had barely started back down to the house when the world began pouring back into his mind. Yesterday. Hugh stopped and looked back. Maybe he'd make an instant coffee in his bedsit rather than fish around for things in the house. Elise was at the gallery and he had the place to himself, but he still preferred to step back a little from the kitchen and the impact of the domestic space going bad. Too many painful memories of his own for sure.

So he turned on his heel and headed over to Jack's side studio. His sketchbooks were in there anyway. He could mull over things. Mix it all up. Wasn't that a good thing? Creativity wasn't just about materials and tools and blocks of stone but the involvement and the confusion of life. Of people. And here he was, down in St. Ives to get away from all that just to find the ubiquity was waiting for him at the other end of the country. Hugh was feeling better able to feel positive about this. He could see how it might all be channeled into the stone. Something deep in him would bring it all together and would inform the Pieta rather than destroy it.

Hugh pushed the door into the side studio and he stepped almost hurriedly past the window toward the desk beneath. He wanted to skim through his sketches from London. Even before sitting down to flick through the pages, he knew they would feel old, distant. A bit hackneyed. He had moved on since then. A slight worry flitted across the front of his mind. Was he ready to break off from concepts and connect to the reality of the stone? At some crucial point, he knew he had to let go of the control and the prediction. All art is improvisation in the making of it. The plans fall away like an airport below the wing. Hugh glanced at the sketches. He thumbed through them and they were now no more relevant or meaningful to him than in-flight safety cards.

• • •

She saw him walk past the gallery window. There was no one else. He wasn't in a hurry. Elise got up and moved to the front of the shop. It suddenly occurred to her that Jonah wasn't in school. She glanced back at the clutter of frames stacked along the wall and in front of the counter. She could leave them. Lock the shop or bring Jonah back in. Without a moment more of indecision, Elise reached out for the door handle.

Jonah was already some yards away and heading down to Fore Street.

"Jonah!" she called. She waited, anxious he wouldn't look back. She was about to call again but Jonah had stopped and turned his head. "Morning." She smiled and waved.

The teenager smiled back and nodded.

"Mrs. Rockshaw. Morning." He turned and began to walk on.

"No, Jonah. Come back. I need to see you."

Already she was following him.

He had stopped. He looked a little puzzled, a little sheepish. She glanced back at the shop just up the lane.

"Jonah. You're not in school. Um, look are you busy? I wanted to ask you something. Tell you about something."

The youth looked at his worn shoes. There was an awkward silence.

"I'm sorry what happened. I was really cross with Simon. Jonah?"

The boy shrugged.

"It's my own fault. No big deal." Jonah looked keen to be getting on. But Elise had him now and wasn't going to let him go so easily. The mother in her took control.

"I want to talk. Come to the shop. Like some tea? Please. Jonah?"

He looked up and nodded vaguely.

"Okay."

"You're not going anywhere are you?"

The boy looked into himself and frowned.

"Not really."

"Good. Come."

She led him back up to the gallery. They reached it soon enough and went in. She closed the door. There'd be no customers this early. And Elise was on her own turf so she felt more confident that she was about to do the right thing.

"Sit. I'll put the kettle on."

Jonah looked uncomfortable. She ignored it. She spoke as she busied herself with mugs and teabags.

"I don't want to talk about the band. It's none of my business. But I'm sorry."

Jonah cleared his throat but kept his mouth shut. He was now sitting on the stool in front of the counter, his knees at an odd angle to avoid the picture frames and samples leaning haphazardly at the side.

"Well anyway. I want you to come over to see Hugh Borne. You know he's staying with us. Did Simon tell you?"

Jonah nodded. He sat up. He didn't seem to know what to say. Elise smiled at him.

"You have talent, Jonah. I'm not doing this because I feel sorry for you. Okay? I was going to ask you over anyway. Um, well, so Hugh is a really nice guy. He's got a son about your age. He'd love to meet you and well . . ." She trailed off. She looked at him for a response. "Would you like to come over?"

"I haven't got a car. Yes, I would. I mean, I would be interested. To see Mr. Borne. I –"

The kettle was boiling and the switch distracted them. Elise turned to finish their tea.

"Great. I'll pick you up. Um, right, well we need to fix a good time. When you're free. How about this weekend? Saturday morning?"

She hadn't asked Hugh. In fact, she hadn't really talked this through with him. But it just felt right. He'd be fine. Her mind was whizzing.

"Okay. Can you pick me up?"

"Of course."

Jonah looked suddenly a little lost. Disconsolate. Elise saw he was trying to work out what she was doing this for.

"Jonah? Sometimes I just do things without thinking too much about them. I just let myself be carried by what I hope are good currents. I know you do that too. You take sugar?"

Jonah nodded.

"How many?"

"Oh. Sorry. No sugar. I was nodding at what you said. I mean, about the sea. No sugar. Thanks."

Elise handed him his mug and sat down on the chair behind the counter. Jonah smiled at last.

"I was talking to Mrs. Jerwood about that yesterday, actually."

Elise watched the boy intently. He hesitated a little under her gaze before continuing.

"You know, about the unconscious. It's so big. It's everything. That's what carries us along. Artists just know how to ride it. Like a wave."

13

"Who, Amy? She just disappeared. We had an impromptu shoot in the afternoon a couple of days back and that was it. She's gone. Hugh? Are you listening? It's not what you think. Come on."

"Elise deserves more than this shit. How can you do this? Jesus Christ, Jack."

"Hey wait a minute. Why are you so determined I'm somehow lying to you? I mean, Hugh, *I'm* not the guy divorced here. I don't need you to put me in the dock on a hunch – because you're feeling sorry for yourself."

"Who is she?"

"Why the interrogation?"

"Elise suspects. I said I'd talk to you. Jack?"

"What?"

"I've been there. We're guys. It doesn't have to be like it was for me. That was different. Don't you love Elise?"

"Wow Hugh. You're insistent, aren't you?"

"But I'm right, aren't I? Come on Jack, face it."

"I'm not going to confess any shit to you."

"Okay. Fine. Give it time. You're back for Christmas but I'd sort it out before then. With *me*. I don't want Elise fucked up about this. Your kids."

"So why's Elise suspect me of having this affair? It's completely random. She's bound to feel anxious. You know, my being out here with a bunch of starry-eyed students."

"Like this Amy girl."

Jack laughed and shook his head.

"No. Oh, Amy's certainly not starry-eyed that's for sure."

There was a pause thousands of miles apart. The two men sat in front of their screens contemplating the situation. The damage. Hugh was happy to be a fellow conspirator if it meant he could patch this up. But he needed Jack to trust him and confess. But Jack could be stubborn. Mean sometimes. Cynical too, when the mood was on him.

"So what do I say?" Hugh asked weakly.

"It's not for you to say anything. Look, Hugh, I appreciate your concern but I'll talk to Elise. I'll talk to her about our conversation. I'll be frank and open. I'll tell her not to worry about Amy. Anyway, the girl's gone. This is a storm in a teacup. It's all about nothing. Elise has to talk to me. I didn't realize there was all this fuss going on behind my back. I know how St. Ives can be. All the gossip. The petty backstabbing. The smallness."

Hugh shook his head.

"Don't be an idiot. She's already seen straight through you. All you're going to do is fuck it up worse for yourself. That's what *I* did. All the lying. The Clinton denial. Don't do it, because it all comes out and you just end up looking like a twat. Okay, look. I don't know. Just don't say anything, sleep on what you know, and . . ."

Hugh broke off. He couldn't look at the screen.

"Hugh? You okay?"

Hugh nodded but didn't look up.

"Sleep on it. Okay? I've got to go. It's two o'clock. I'm knackered. Night Jack."

"Sure. Okay. Goodnight. It'll be fine."

Hugh reached up and closed the connection. Jack's face froze then the screen went blank.

"Sure it will."

• • •

Jonah walked back to Fore Street and on toward the harbor. He could see the red and blue fishing boats sat snug on the high tide tethered to fluorescent orange buoys or rusty iron rings along the quay. As he emerged from Back Lane and wandered past the Sloop Inn, the bay of the town opened to him and, out beyond Smeaton's Pier and Wheal Dream, the horizon of the land arched round to the Hayle estuary and Gwithian far off.

Jonah tried to ignore the gnawing guilt of not being in school. He wanted to feel free but it was impossible. He walked around the harbor toward Quay Street, keeping his head down. Fearing exposure. Mrs. Rockshaw had gone on about his being out. Someone from school might see him. It wasn't good feeling so uncovered. But he wanted to get to the pier. He wanted to look out over the gray sea beyond the town where Alfred Wallis's cardboard three masters were sailing back from the Grand Banks of Newfoundland or the Grimsby trawlers were lurking far off between the crab pots and the horizon. Only Wallis could paint boats. Capture the solitude of it all. He had lived it and that was his trick. The artist should never use his imagination. Just experience.

• • •

Amy emerged from the South Ferry subway and crossed State Street for Battery Park. She walked with conviction, like she knew where she was going. There was an icy wind ripping off Upper Bay and it throttled the black branches free of their final specks of coiled brown leaves. They were flicked in ones and twos, spiraling back toward the ferry terminals and the toe-end blocks of Manhattan. Two gulls were fast elbowed out the way by the lumpy gusts of wind that tore your breath.

Amy pulled the zipper up on her jacket and pushed back her flailing fair hair. She marched on toward the far west side of the park and the view that opened out over the Hudson, past the islands far out to The Narrows.

It was just about the only place she could breathe; where you weren't eyeballing a wall. It was the nearest she could get to a hillside looking out. She had come here to get away from Jack. She had come here to escape all that creative shit and the relentless turbine of the ego driving and imposing. Stubborn, obsessive, deaf, and blind. Ceaselessly chattering and tugging at your sleeve for attention. Art was loveless. Artful. And she realized how much she hated it because it was humanity disguised as something better than it was. She wished New Jersey wasn't there staring back at her like some dumb fuck.

She watched the boats in the fading light of the afternoon. She followed the lugubrious progress of a dredger right to the point it was eaten by Ellis Island. But it was too cold to linger more and she still wanted to walk back up through the park. Take the subway at Bowling Green. So she turned her back on the brown sea with its flecks of white and the wide foam fantails behind the tugs and the ferries and she headed away from the promenade northward between the bare trees.

• • •

Koenig's Sphere was taken in pieces to the salvage yard at JFK shortly after 9/11. Fritz Koenig waited five months before the fractured metal fragments were pasted back and the shattered orb was placed in Battery Park. A fallen star. Gargarin's Vostok I all punched up and slung out. A bashed in skull. Dented ego.

Amy walked slowly around it. Once a corporate fountain, a ball of commercial crap had been metamorphosed into a reluctant work of iconic art. So here was the secret to it all. But now that Koenig's baby had grown up to have meaning and a reason, no one wanted it. The Port Authorities planned to move the old hobo out. Actually, that's what it was. A hobo staggering toward us between the truth and the shame of being human. Maybe it would disappear overnight stolen for scrap metal like Hepworth's Divided Circle. Jack had told her about that. It was a tragedy. A million dollars' worth of bronze melted down for a few greenbacks. She had thought it hilarious. Not the theft so much but the way he had talked about the money not the value. Like a piece of art was just where money and ego came together like egg and sperm. And the product of the procreative act must never grow up to have a meaningful life of her own. Such proud and possessive parents.

Amy stepped back and stared up at the tired ball.

"There should be a boneyard in the Mojave for all you guys. I'll come and hang out with you. Live in my painted plane."

• • •

Wikipedia

Damien Hirst

"I can't wait to get into a position to make really bad art and get away with it. At the moment if I did certain things people would look at it, consider it and then say 'f off'. But after a while you can get away with things."

"The thing about 9/11 is that it's kind of like an artwork in its own right. It was wicked, but it was devised in this way for this kind of impact. It was devised visually. . . You've got to hand it to them on some level because they've achieved something which nobody would have ever have thought possible, especially to a country as big as America. So on one level they kind of need congratulating, which a lot of people shy away from, which is a very dangerous thing."

He is internationally renowned, and is reportedly Britain's richest living artist, with his wealth valued at £215m in the 2010 Sunday Times Rich List.

• • •

Hugh Borne

Hugh Borne
Born 14 June 1962
Poole, Dorset, United Kingdom
British sculptor, painter

Hugh Borne is a British artist known for his figurative work in stone and for his portraits in oils. He is best known for his sculptures inspired by the poetry of John Clare and the later works of Turner. He has consistently produced works in stone, mixed media, and oils that many would describe as 'primitivist'. His exhibition 'Primitivism' at The Tate St. Ives (2002), was received with critical acclaim and resulted in the showing of 'Virgin Rock' and 'Shore' at New York's Museum of Modern Art 'Anti-Anti-Art' exhibition of British and American remodernists (2005). Hugh Borne is a member of the Stuckist group of British artists and his work has been on view at the Stuckist International Centre and Gallery in Shoreditch, London since 2003. Since joining the movement, Hugh Borne has actively participated in protests at the Tate Britain against the Turner Prize and is a vociferous critic of the Saatchi Gallery and the Young British Artists (YBA).

• • •

"*Michel?*"

"*Oui. J'arrive. Un moment.*"

"Michael?"

"I'm coming."

Michael heard his mother in the entrée opening the apartment door. His uncle and aunt had arrived. He closed the screen of his laptop and sighed. He heard adult voices outside his door. His mother's high heels clip-clopping across the parquet floor. There was a knock and his mother came into his bedroom without waiting.

"*Michel? Ton oncle est arrivé. Viens, mon cher.*"

Michael rose from his chair. He glanced back at the computer to check it was charging.

"*Et Christelle est ici. Ils sont tout à fait mourir de toi rencontrer.*"

"*D'ac.*"

"*Est-toi heureux, Michel?*"

"*Oui*." Michael shrugged. He was keen for them both to leave his space. He didn't want some sort of drama. He saw his mother glance at the laptop. She frowned.

"*Tu sembles triste*."

Michael shook his head a little defiantly.

"*Ce n'est rien. Ce n'est pas grave. Maman*."

"*Ton père? Tu veux* – "

"*Non. Jamais*."

• • •

Jack got back to the apartment late. The subway had been packed with tourists, Christmas shoppers heading back from Uptown, gray-faced students, mums and dads with overwrought kids all close to melt-down. He was exhausted. The Christmas thing was a fucking nightmare. Brainless. Mad. But the whole time, from Fifty-Ninth Street to Bleecker, he could only think of Amy. He had the final prints all mounted and framed back at the Faculty. He had visualized their looking at them together; deciding which they thought were best, over a bottle or two of wine. He wanted to see her looking at the images of herself. Naked. Transformed into a bodyscape by light and shadows. Ethereal.

He opened the apartment door and pushed through with his foot, his hands full – he'd been to the Apple Store for the kids – keys in his mouth. He switched on the entrance light with his elbow. And he just wanted to let the whole lot cascade to the ground. Smash to bits.

14

Christmas was just two weeks away and stood waiting like the Dark Monarch on the Zennor moors.

• • •

Jonah sat uncomfortably in the Rockshaw's kitchen, his school sketchbook on his knees. Mrs. Rockshaw had left him to find Mr. Borne. There was a mug of coffee at his elbow on the kitchen table. Quite apart from wondering what the hell he was doing here, was the worry that Simon or even Caja would suddenly come in and just see this guy sitting in their kitchen like a complete dork. He could see Simon's eyes narrow with suspicion. He'd say nothing, slip out and the next thing, Jonah would hear his voice calling for his mum, wanting to know what was going on.

Jonah blinked the imaginings away as best he could. He heard voices outside. Adult ones near the house. They were getting closer and then he heard the porch door opening and the vibration in the floor connecting them somehow. Even then, the kitchen door from the porch opened too suddenly and it startled him.

"Jonah's just here."

"Right," came a man's voice.

Jonah began to rise. And there they were: Mrs. Rockshaw and Mr. Borne filling what had been empty space.

"Hello Jonah. Elise has been telling me all about you."

"Hi. Mr. Borne. Um –"

"Is that your work?" the man asked abruptly.

Jonah looked at the sketchbook in his hands. He felt a little guilty.

There was an awkward pause for a second. Mrs. Rockshaw smiled.

"Hugh, you want something to drink?"

Mr. Borne glanced at her and shook his head.

"Thanks. No, I'm fine. Here, Jonah. May I?" He held out his hand for the book. It was a gesture of friendship. Jonah could tell he was genuinely interested.

"Sure. It's just my sketchbook. For my final exams. It's nothing really." He handed his work to Mr. Borne, who took it and went to sit at the table. His eyes were on the book, not the chair he was pulling out. Mrs. Rockshaw seemed to have left them to it. Jonah felt her deliberately step herself away so they could talk. He felt every move, every gesture with acute shyness. He hesitated to sit down and hovered stupidly. He watched Mr. Borne looking. The artist turned the pages slowly. He began to nod.

"See, Hugh? Good, isn't he?"

Mr. Borne nodded and frowned. Jonah didn't know why, but he just felt like he wanted to melt into the floor.

After a while, Mr. Borne looked up and seemed almost to shake his head as if he'd forgotten something.

"Hey, I'm sorry. Jonah. Hi. I'm Hugh. Pleased to meet you."

With that, the artist reached out his hand across the table.

"Hi. I'm glad to meet you Mr. Borne." Jonah stepped forward and shook the proffered hand. The grip was surprisingly powerful. The skin was dry. He felt the large bones, the nub of knuckle.

"Jonah's into Sven Berlin," came Mrs. Rockshaw's voice from the other side of the kitchen. Jonah made to sit at the table.

"Yes. I see that," replied Mr. Borne. He glanced at the book and it seemed to draw him again. "Love these owls. They're fun." He nodded as he looked and turned the pages once more. "They're good."

Jonah began to relax. The shame was sliding to one side.

"Mrs. Jerwood is my art teacher. We have to keep this sketchbook. She told us to look at da Vinci's notebooks. His sketches and stuff."

Mr. Borne looked up. He nodded.

"Sure. But remember, Leonardo da Vinci took what he could. I mean, there were no exams. He learned on the hoof. With artists. Mentors. Verrocchio. People like that. Same with Sven Berlin. The system is a system. That's all. Artists work on the outside. Stay aloof. Remember, there have always been artists. The education system has only been around since the industrial revolution. Know what I'm saying? Learn art from artists not school teachers. Feed your art on life."

Mrs. Rockshaw came over. Jonah noticed how she caught Mr. Borne's eye. The sculptor leaned back. His chair creaked.

"I'll tell you something, Jonah. I went to all the right schools. Falmouth then onto the Slade. I'm a thoroughly tutored artist. It has given me contacts, maybe. It's given me a comfortable ride, I suppose. But I couldn't do *this* when I was your age. What does your art teacher say to you?"

Jonah felt confused. He shrugged.

"Dunno. She said I might get a 'B' but my coursework's behind."

Mr. Borne looked up at Mrs. Rockshaw standing there listening and he shook his head.

"Beware. You are entering the world of the critical eyes that watch you and so many will seek your destruction. The art world is driven by greed and egos. It's a world that sets out to destroy talent. Never immerse yourself in this thing. The great artist, the genius, is a cursed man because no one will bless him. Not until he's dead, at least."

"Oh Hugh," came Mrs. Rockshaw's voice. She moved away as if disappointed.

"It's true. Tell it how it is, Elise."

"I don't think Jonah needs to hear all that," she replied almost over her shoulder.

"It's all right, Mrs. Rockshaw," Jonah found himself saying. He was so sensitive to adult disagreements. Fights. He looked at Mr. Borne.

"I've seen enough already. I know what it's like. I'm not a kid." He looked at his sketchbook on the table between Mr. Borne's elbows. "I put it all in there. You know. I don't give a shit what people think. It's not why I draw stuff."

Mr. Borne smiled at him.

"Sure." He raised his finger. "Don't chase money. Money is poison. It will destroy you. *This* is what you have." He pointed at the book. "You don't need anything else other than self-absorption."

• • •

Elise peered around the door.

"Jonah's here," she said.

Hugh looked up and saw the warm smile. The tired eyes.

"Great." He lowered his iPad and pushed back his chair. "Elise?"

"What?"

"What do you want me to say?" He really wanted to ask what she was doing. What did she want him to do? He reached the door and Elise had already stepped out into the cold damp air. She was waiting on the grassy path, her back at an angle to him.

"Elise?"

"Just talk to the boy. He needs a boost." She looked around as Hugh closed the door. "Anyway, he's good, Hugh. He has real talent and sensitivity and well, maybe just take that and see what happens."

They began to walk to the house side by side. Hugh didn't look up. He was thoughtful.

"And look, he's been going through a rough patch. His father walked out on them last year. Mum's a boozer."

"Oh."

"Hugh, I'm not doing this because I feel sorry for him."

"You know, did anyone ever show interest in your talent, your creativity? I mean, when you were this age?" he asked.

Elise stopped.

"Of course not."

Hugh shook his head.

"Everyone's against it, aren't they? Parents worry. Think you're going to get into drugs. It's an egomaniac teenage phase to be grown out of."

Elise smiled.

"Maybe they were right. So, what? Are you going to tell Jonah to grow up and get a proper job?"

Hugh shrugged.

"Has it made us happy? What is the benefit of hindsight?"

Elise began to walk on. She was getting cold and didn't want to leave Jonah languishing in the kitchen.

"You don't have to be happy. Just realize you'd be more miserable sitting in an office dreaming of being an artist."

• • •

Wikipedia

Banksy

On 21 February 2007, Sotheby's auction house in London auctioned three works, reaching the highest ever price for a Banksy work at auction: over £102,000 for his Bombing Middle England. Two of his other graffiti works, Balloon Girl and Bomb Hugger, sold for £37,200 and £31,200 respectively, which were well above their estimated prices. The following day's auction saw a further three Banksy works reach soaring prices: Ballerina with Action Man Parts reached £96,000; Glory sold for £72,000; Untitled (2004) sold for £33,600; all significantly above estimated values. To coincide with the second day of auctions, Banksy updated his website with a new image of an auction house scene showing people bidding on a picture that said, "I Can't Believe You Morons Actually Buy This Shit." In February 2007, the owners of a house with a Banksy mural on the side in Bristol decided to sell the house through Red Propeller art gallery after offers fell through because the prospective buyers wanted to remove the mural. It is listed as a mural that comes with a house attached. In 2008, Nathan Wellard and Maev Neal, a couple from Norfolk, UK, made headlines in Britain when they decided to sell their mobile home that contains a 30-foot mural, entitled Fragile Silence, done by Banksy a decade prior to his rise to fame. According to Nathan Wellard, Banksy had asked the couple if he could use the side of their home as a "large canvas," to which they agreed. In return for the "canvas", the Bristol stencil artist gave them two free tickets to the Glastonbury Music Festival. The mobile home purchased by the couple 11 years ago for 1,000 GBP, is now being sold for 500,000 GBP.

• • •

"Amy?"

She must have sat in on the class. Everyone had gone. It was his last class of the semester. She was sitting at the back. She looked bored.

"Happy Christmas. I missed you." Jack wanted to play it cool. He shuffled papers on his desk and started closing the programs on his laptop. The image of Rembrandt's *The Woman Taken in Adultery* disappeared suddenly from the projector screen. There was an interval of silence. Jack frowned to himself. How should he play this? He looked up.

"You okay?"

The room echoed slightly with her cough.

"I'm good. Enjoyed the class. The Rembrandt was a joke, right?"

Jack glanced back at the blank screen.

"Not really. Not a joke exactly. But . . ." he shrugged, "you know. Stops me from getting tired of it all. You going back to Long Island? See your parents?"

"Do I have to?"

Jack lowered the papers in his hand. His shoulder twitched again.

"Um, I guess not." He smiled as if remembering something. "Actually, yes you do. Christmas dictates and says you've got to go and be a child once more. It's about love and commitment. It's family Hajj. Besides, don't you want to?"

"No. No more than anyone. It's a stolen convention."

Jack didn't know how to answer. He just sighed.

"Sure. Um, I suppose I'm all done here. Did you want to go somewhere?" He switched off the microphone and some lights that left him in shadow.

"Sounds okay."

"I wanted to show you the prints. They're stunning. I mean, *you're* stunning. Amy, are you mad at me about something? I'll confess you've got me confused."

"What with?"

"Okay, well, that's for you to say. Oh come on, let's get out of here. I'm wasting valuable recess time. Let's go find an inn for the night."

"Jack?"

"What?"

"I do everything to escape; I mean the things I want to do – the things you do so you don't spend life just dying away the days. I fuck to escape, I drink, I wander, I gate crash your class, I wander some more only to get out. I'm not a butterfly. You said that once. Yeah? I'm not a butterfly, Jack. I'm not looking for knowledge or understanding from flower to flower. I'm trying to find the exit door in a black room."

"I'll drink to that. Every day is one day closer, one stroke farther from the shore."

"That a quote?"

"It is now."

15

"I'm not having a midlife crisis. God, I hate it when people say that. Look, I just love her. It's so rare. It's never happened before. I want you to meet her. I want Elise to meet her. You'd all understand why I'm doing this."

Hugh sat stunned. He was still stuck at the point when Jack said he wasn't returning for Christmas and it all came out.

"Hugh?"

"Yeah, I'm still here."

"Thought you'd frozen."

Hugh moved and looked back up at the screen.

"Well, no one's going to impeach you, I suppose. How old is she?"

"She's wise, Hugh. It's like she's got all the hindsight ahead of her."

"How are you going to tell Elise?"

"I'm sending her an e-mail. Tell her everything. Maybe we can talk it through after."

"Great. Thanks. Shit, Jack. Look, I can't take this in. What are you doing? You're nuts."

"Of course you don't get it. This whole thing is so out of your frame of reference."

"No Jack. Wrong. Half the picture's over here with me. Fuck. At least do this after Christmas. I mean, Jesus. How old is she? How ridiculous are you being?"

"She's at NYU. Hugh it's –"

"Student. Twenty-nothing. What the fuck are you doing?!"

"Okay, okay. I knew this was a bad idea. Look, I got to go. I'll e-mail Elise. Just keep out of this. I'll deal with –"

"No wait. Keep out of this? Jack, what are you going on about? No, Jack, don't. Wait . . ."

• • •

Elise,

I don't know how to begin. I wanted to Skype but thought I'd write first. I can't get back for Christmas. I spoke to Hugh and I've thought very hard about all this and that you need to know probably sooner rather than later. I can't explain anything here but I think we need a divorce. Maybe I'm having a sort of breakdown. I don't know. Yes, there's an affair. All very tedious and I'm the bastard. I'm sorry. Of course I will support you and the kids and all that. It's best that we talk this through and sort it out ourselves. If the lawyers take over, they'll have us fighting until there's nothing. Let's not do that. I hope you will write back without too much anger and hurt and that we can sort out the future. Let's please be amicable and set a good example to Simon and Caja. When you're ready, we should Skype. We need to talk this through.

Take care,

Jack

• • •

"The little prick."

• • •

"You did what?! Are you out of your mind?! Christ, Jack, you're old enough to be my dad!"

"What the hell's *that* supposed to mean? Can you keep your voice down? People are looking at us."

Amy glanced over her shoulder. There were two guys on rollerblades about to pass them. She moved closer to him – maybe a little reluctantly.

They both stopped and looked at each other as if for the first time. Amy shook her head and began to smile. Then she laughed and raised her arm. She lifted caught hair out of her coat hood with a hand scoop. It struck Jack as a rather confident gesture.

"Okay," she said, lowering her hand and leaning forward. She raised a finger at him. "This is your life. *Your* life. This here. This is *my* life. My life. See?" With that, she swung her foot forward and drew an imaginary line between them with her toe. Then she turned away.

"Shit . . ."

She started walking on.

"Amy? Amy, wait. Amy, listen to me. I haven't finished."

Jack strode out to catch her up. He came alongside, hands shoved deep into his coat pockets. The wind had died in the last day or so but the gray air was icy. Felt like snow.

"Why'd you have to go and screw it up?" she asked without looking at him.

"Listen. This isn't what you think. This isn't about us. You know, 'us'. Can we slow down, please?"

Amy shrugged. She did slow. Just a little.

"Look, I was going to do this anyway. Sure, I value your freedom. I value it more than your friendship. Well, so you'd better value mine too."

Amy glanced at him with sharp blue eyes.

"I value that, Jack. Line's for both of us."

"I know. Look, this may sound harsh, but if I hadn't found you, I'd have found someone else."

The blue eyes went from narrow to wide, wide. Amy started picking up her City pace like she was heading for the subway.

Suddenly Jack stopped. He realized how fast they had been walking, when he saw Amy sailing off, unraveling the distance between them with an invisible thread.

He stood and watched her go. Something in him rejoiced. It was that she didn't slow for him. She just kept on walking. But it was more than that. He began to laugh to himself. Tonight's fucking was going to be the best ever.

He turned and headed back toward Columbus Square with a sigh and a slight spring in his step.

• • •

"When did you know?"

"Why don't you come in? Close the door."

Elise frowned and stepped into the studio bedsit reluctantly.

"It's like he's turned into a big kid. Oh Hugh . . ."

Elise closed the door and just stood there looking rather lost. Hugh watched her carefully for the signs of where she was. What should he say?

Neither spoke. Then both spoke at once, interrupting each other.

"I'm –"

"Sorry –"

"You go first."

Hugh looked down.

"What did he say in the e-mail?" he asked.

"Nothing really."

Elise stepped further into the room. She didn't seem that distressed – like she was going to cry – and it didn't look as though she had been crying. Hugh couldn't detect self-pity and the anger was tired. He'd make sure he helped keep her away from all that.

"I almost feel guilty," he said.

Elise half-smiled.

"Funny. I was going to say the same thing."

"Oh?"

"Hardly what you need right now. I mean, with your work," she said.

"It's nothing. It's life. Look, um, should I go back up to London? Keep out the way . . . over Christmas?"

The question was sort of a test. See how she would react.

A shadow flicked briefly across her brow. She frowned more with thought than upset.

"Do you *want* to leave?"

"No. Not really. Unless it was to India or somewhere."

Elise gave a wan smile.

"Sure. We'd all love to escape. If he'd told me sooner, we could have booked flights. Now we're stuck with god-awful Christmas. That was nice of him."

"I'm sorry."

"Don't say that. I hate it. Look, I'm sort of not surprised. Maybe it happened before. At least he's being honest now. It's out in the open and we can stop pretending. I'm not even frightened. He's not an evil man, Hugh. Just human. Like you."

Hugh shifted uneasily. She wanted to carry on and he was earnest about wanting to listen, to play the counselor, the confessor.

"I'm not sad, or angry, you know, about the – you know – the betrayal, I suppose. But it's still sad, like it's a shame it has to be like this. Why do we all set ourselves up – I mean, the expectations that things will be different, the world will change?

"How old is she? Do you know anything about her?"

The last questions were sudden. Hugh was a little startled. He really didn't want to say. Elise was calm, wasn't she? Keep it that way. He shrugged.

"Jack was pretty guarded. You know, it wasn't easy for him. I don't mean he should . . . I mean, I don't think he felt able to go on about it. He's obviously ashamed."

"Is it a fling?"

Hugh didn't know how to answer. He kept quiet. Elise answered for him.

"No. Of course it's not. He wouldn't have told me. The divorce. Sure." She nodded to herself. "I suppose that's what really hurts. I *wish* it was just a fling. Casual fuck with one of his students. Suppose I've been dumped, haven't I?"

Hugh detected a change of mood. They were beginning to sail close to the self-pity he so dreaded.

"You will tell me what he says. Don't keep things from me, Hugh. Secrets don't protect, they exclude. You knew about this before, didn't you? And you're keeping things from me. That's unkind. It's cowardly."

Hugh rose from his chair at the desk, his sketches laid out in front of him in a disorderly pile. He shook his head in protest but it was pretense, of course. He realized that and felt annoyed with himself.

"Of course. No, I won't try to protect you. Look, this is difficult for me too. I didn't know this was going to happen. I knew nothing. I wouldn't have come down had I known this was all going to blow up."

Elise folded her arms.

"So you want to go back to London then?" She spoke half affirmatively.

"No. Not now. It's too late. That's not what I'm saying. I just didn't ask for this anymore than you. I'm caught in the middle."

"He trusts you."

"Sort of. He's used me, in a way. Hoping I'll pass things on like a PA. Bloody insulting, really."

"Sure. He's an arrogant shit."

They both looked at each other almost as if a penny had dropped.

• • •

"We'll go to Oyster Bay. Mom's in DC."

Amy spoke as she pulled at Jack's belt. He looked down at her busy fingers. There was a fraught annoyance in the way she tugged at his fly. Like an addict or a pissed-off mother with a naughty child.

"Sounds good. We don't have a car."

Amy didn't answer. Her visual spatial sketchpad was all booked up. His own frame of reference was pretty much engorged too. Jack watched the back of Amy's head as it sank in the dressing table mirror behind her. He stared back at himself as she tugged down the side of his pants with one hand, pulling him out with the other. The last thing he noticed, before they fell back onto the bed behind, was her T-shirt still draped over the end of the dresser.

• • •

Jonah sat on the end of his bed. He was staring out of the window. He couldn't see the roofs of the other houses on the estate – he was too low down – just the lumpy gray of a sky that had lost the will to be bright ever. There were three seagulls quite high up: little stiff planes falling sideways.

It was the second Christmas without his dad. Everything broken of course. He sat feeling like he was just hanging on; still a bit of a kid at the beach: blob of vanilla ice cream melting on the sand at his feet, empty cone in hand, wondering what to do. He remembered that afternoon just then, oddly. He hadn't cried like a normal kid. He hadn't complained or asked for another. He just had this overwhelming feeling of having lost something perhaps important. It was a premonition of course. That's why he was recalling the moment now.

He could hear the Band Aid Christmas song on the TV downstairs. With a sigh, he leaned back on the bed and just lay there – ceiling replacing sky – and he took his mind back to Zennor, the barn, the great stone. Then he gently closed his eyes and went to sleep.

THE PIETA, 1498-1499
MICHELANGELO

JANUARY

16

Somehow they had all got through Christmas. Jack spent five days in Oyster Bay with his head buried in Amy. Hugh didn't go to New York, or London, or India. Elise had coped. She hadn't told the children what was going on. There was a time for such a thing. She had written to tell Jack it was up to him to let his kids know what he thought he was doing. If he believed it was right so much, he'd have no problem facing Simon and Caja and informing them – instructing them on the rights and wrongs, the ins and outs, and the whys and wherefores of adultery and family abandonment. Certainly she wasn't going to pick up the shit he'd left behind, etcetera . . .

Time is not a great healer, but memory learns to forget and pain gets pushed to the periphery. It takes exactly two weeks for a human being to let diurnal minutiae elbow even the most cataclysmic disasters to the edges of attention, working memory, recent history recall. Two weeks and wine.

Jonah had visited the Rockshaws during the Christmas holidays almost daily. He caught the bus to St. Just from the bottom of the Stennack in St. Ives and walked up from the bus stop at Zennor. Hugh would drive him back in Jack's car.

He had sat and watched Hugh prepare the stone for cutting. They would leave the barn door open to the elements, Jonah leaning back against the doorway half looking on, half looking out over the stooped hag hedges and the winter cold sea. At first it was odd to Hugh, that the boy would come like a stray off the moors and sit there politely. Sometimes shivering. But he soon accepted it and he spoke less because the boy said little. Perhaps it was shyness or sensitivity.

When he needed to rest his hands and he had to stop for ten minutes, sometimes half an hour (the tendons and sinews in his fingers and wrists throbbing enough to bring tears), they might talk. Jonah would make them coffee. When Hugh was cutting with the power tools, Jonah had sat outside.

But the real reason silence had joined them was because Christmas was a black ocean at the bottom of an abyss. Vast. Grotesque.

They had clung to the barn like marooned sailors on a spit of land. They were survivors in a retreat from the pestilence watching themselves for the first symptoms, and all the while glancing out to the beyond and the house down the path.

• • •

"God. I've got to rest. My hands are stumps. Look at that," said Hugh holding up the chisel.

Jonah looked back. He'd been staring out to sea. Miles away.

Hugh sniffed and wiped a dewdrop off the end of his nose with the back of his upturned wrist, the point of the chisel close to his right ear.

"You making coffee?" Hugh lowered his arm and half dropped the chisel on the trestle table he'd drawn up close for his tools. He winced with pain and shook his head. He was tired and a bit irritable.

Jonah was blurred; there was stone dust in the air, but he saw the boy get to his feet and stand, framed by the open door and the gray light. Hugh raised his hand and removed his eye protection. Jonah stirred.

"Sorry. I was dreaming. I'll go get some. Can I see?" He moved from the door and approached. He didn't look at Hugh. Just the stone, now so mauled and ripped. Hugh watched him, or rather the green eyes roving over his work. The boy was locked into the stone. Hugh now glanced at the rock himself. What did the boy see? For some minutes they stood watching, as if searching.

"What is it?" asked Hugh.

"Huh?" Jonah blinked and stepped back. "Um, it's nothing."

Hugh stepped round.

"Yes. There's something you want to say. Say it."

The boy reddened and shook his head.

"No. I'll go make the coffee."

"Listen. This . . . this thing . . ." Hugh looked at the stone. "This is not an ego. You know? I mean, if you want to say something, say it."

The boy shook his head and looked more uncomfortable.

"I know. I can't."

"Can we start communicating, Jonah – I mean blunt stuff?"

The boy frowned.

"Blunt? Whatd'ya mean?"

"Go make the coffee. My hands are fucked. We'll talk when you get back. That okay?"

Jonah shrugged and looked puzzled. He frowned.

"Sure. All right."

• • •

It was a bright, ice-cold morning. Amy and Jack were crossing the railroad near the sports club off Shore Street. The sky was electric blue with smudges of gray clouds high over the harbor and the Long Island Sound, like distant smoke signals. Jack was bleary. He winced at the winter light even though they'd been out half an hour or so. They passed the boathouses down West End Avenue and headed across the parking lot to the beach and the crystal water. Amy wanted to talk art. Jack kept up like he did, but his brief responses and comments were an indifferent accompaniment. He felt a poor companion that morning.

"New York *made* Saul Leiter, don't you think?" Amy said, stepping neatly off the end of the slipway onto the white beach. There was a light frost and the sand was firm under her dark blue canvass shoes.

"Saul Leiter? Whatd'ya mean?" Jack joined her alongside. There were four sailing dinghies tugging at the slim breeze just offshore. They slipped westward like swans. Jack was transported, briefly, to Falmouth.

"If there had been no New York, there'd have been no Saul Leiter. Places make people, not the other way around."

"Maybe. I guess he'd not have done the same sort of stuff if he'd been in Paris. Or London."

"Hmm."

"A good artist, especially a photographer, knows how to bring out a place. You know, exploit it."

"Sure. Or a person. Responding, not imposing."

"Leave imposing to architects. Artists don't create environments, they deal with them."

Amy was half listening. She wandered on ahead and wanted to sit somewhere. She redirected them back around toward the beach road and a line of winter black trees. They could sit on the edge over there.

"Jack?"

"What?"

"Do you feel bad?"

"Bad? What about?"

Amy glanced back at him and gave him a skeptical smile.

"Not going back. Your family. Remember them? Your folks. Home?"

There was a mocking tone Jack didn't much care for. He shrugged and looked away. The boats had reached the end of the beach and leaned a little. They were more strung out.

"There's nothing more I can say. We've talked about all that."

They had reached the trees and the edge of the asphalt. There was a good ledge for sitting. Amy swept the surface with her gloved hand before she pulled herself up and sat. Her feet hung down an inch above the sand. Jack joined her and they sat watching the sea and the boats without a word for a minute or so before Jack spoke.

"Of course I feel bad. Do you feel bad that I feel bad?"

Amy smiled.

"There'd be no altruism, no pity without guilt. Positive acts depend on such negativity. It's like you can't be creative unless the world is falling apart. Maybe you fucked up your life on me just for the inspiration. Squeeze out one more show."

Jack laughed. He didn't reply. He wanted to savor the hurt and not engage with Amy. He felt she was bored with him. She'd provoke and play games when she was uninspired.

She looked at him and leaned her shoulder against his, placing her hand down between his thighs.

"I didn't thank you, did I?" she said in a peppery whisper.

"What for?"

"Adding me to your collection. You could make me vain hanging me up on walls like that. I'd hate it – to be weakened by your adoration."

She slipped her hand up and felt him stiffen.

Jack sighed.

• • •

Hugh pressed his sore fingers around the mug to get a little heat into his joints. The coffee vapor spiraled up into the dank chill air of the studio.

"I read some stuff," Jonah said.

The two of them were back standing before the cut rock. Elise had phoned from the gallery. She had asked if Hugh would join her for a drink after work. Maybe Jonah could come too. They had agreed to meet in the Sloop.

"What did you read?"

"About the Pieta."

Hugh nodded and they both looked at the stone.

"And?" Hugh asked. He needed to prompt the shy youth.

"Well, first they're all the same. Basically."

Hugh nodded.

"Iconography rather than art. Like angels on tombstones."

Jonah didn't reply but seemed to be considering Hugh's remark. He let it go.

"But what happened to Joseph?"

"Which one?"

Jonah looked at him.

"The dad."

Hugh looked back from the rock and smiled.

"Ah. Well, now there's a thing. It's scriptural rather than sculptural. I mean, he buggered off when Christ was twelve. Apparently."

"Did he die? What happened to him?"

Hugh frowned. There was an intensity lacking humor in Jonah's voice.

"Well, the Bible doesn't say. Or if it did, it was cut out in one of the many translations over the years. The fact is, when Jesus started saying he was the son of God, I guess Joseph felt it was time to pack his bags. Poor Joseph." Hugh allowed himself to linger on the thought for a moment. The cuckold father. A cuckoo God. "Joseph was written out. God made him redundant and, anyway, the people who wrote the Bible must have thought he was rather inconvenient. Maybe Jesus thought so too. So he had to go. Anyway. He wasn't the dad. I mean . . . it's all nonsense."

Jonah lowered the mug in his hand.

"But it's how people think."

"Whatd'ya mean?"

"You know, like Jung and Greek myths. The stories are important because they show us how we think."

Hugh nodded.

"Or else they tell us. Well, maybe it's true. I mean, dads are crap. All that matters are mothers. The church needs them to swell the ranks and do the homework. *They're* the storm troopers, not the priests." Hugh stepped toward the rock. A particular cut had caught his eye and he was momentarily distracted. He reached out and flicked something near the emerging head of Mary. "Do you think we should stick a dad in? I hadn't planned for that." He looked back at Jonah and smiled.

"Of course not."

"To be honest, I've got no real say in this. I'm no more than a stonemason. It's for a convent school."

Jonah looked surprised.

"Really?"

Hugh nodded and went to put his mug on the tool table.

"Sure." He saw the disappointment in Jonah's eyes.

"A convent?"

"Yep. Jonah, I'm not religious. This means nothing more to me than a payment." He looked down. "That's how it is."

"It's not art, then, is it?" said Jonah uncertainly. Hugh felt the boy was confused at the sudden realization, the disappointment, and the lie of it all.

"Maybe it's more craft. It's creative. Artwork is something very different. It's the easiest thing in the world and the hardest. It's what we do best but it's done only really for ourselves. Sometimes someone comes over and asks what you're doing, and you look up and shrug your shoulders. That's art. It does its thing and it doesn't care."

"But I thought you were really into this." Jonah's face was a puzzled mask.

"I love the stone. The material is the most important thing – for a sculptor. This allows me to play with my favorite things but the idea? The soul if it . . .?" Hugh shook his head. "It's nothing really."

Hugh was lying. It was sort of where he had got to but not where he wanted to be. He coughed and sighed.

"I didn't want it to be like this. Sure. It doesn't have to be all one or the other. I've given up on this one. I need the money, that's all and I lost the way. There. You have my confession."

Hugh moved away from the boy and looked for his chisels. The eye protectors.

"Best get on. I need to finish this corner. Another hour, then we'll take you back. You're okay about joining us at the pub?"

Jonah was still lost in his thoughts but managed to nod back.

"Sure, that'll be nice. Thanks."

17

"One cider. Looks a bit cloudy to me. Shall I take it back?

"No it's fine. It's a sort of Cornish scrumpy."

"Oh right." Hugh sat himself at the table. The pub was quiet. Elise was looking out of the small window onto the harbor front. She seemed a little distant.

"Do you want crisps or something?" he asked.

She shook her head and looked around.

"I'm all right. You get some if you want."

"Not bothered. Cheers." Hugh raised his pint and took a modest sip.

"Is Jonah okay?"

"Yes. He changed his mind on the way down. I think he's still keen to keep out of Simon's way. Said he had some school work."

Elise frowned.

"Well, he shouldn't worry about Simon. None of Simon's business, is it?"

Hugh looked at his beer.

"No. Sure. I suppose you're right. He's a sensitive boy."

"Who, Simon?"

"No, Jonah."

"Yes. Yes, he is. Simon takes after his father." Elise sighed with exasperation.

"Jonah was quite helpful today, actually," said Hugh, keen to pull away from any references to Jack.

"Oh?" Elise said, taking her cider and raising it.

"Yes. Actually, I like having him around. I didn't at first. You know, off-putting. But he keeps to himself a bit like a cat and then sidles over when he knows I'm taking a break and he says this or that and I value it. I think it's because he's young. He sees so much I don't."

"Like what?" Elise began to look more interested. She took another swig before lowering her glass.

"Oh, I don't know. Um, well, like today . . ." Hugh hesitated when he realized it was a touchy subject – Joseph, the missing father. He stumbled on. "Let me think . . . Oh, yes, we talked a little about conventional forms, religious icons. I think he was a bit down when I ranted on about, well, the less creative aspects of what I do." Hugh looked up and shrugged. "His disappointment is a sort of reminder."

"Is it?" Elise leaned back and Hugh could see she was happy to disagree.

"Well, you know. Anyway, it's good to have a young perspective hanging around," he added weakly.

"You so wanted this to work, Hugh. Remember how on edge you were before Christmas? You've given in. You started this project young and now you're old. Like me."

Hugh laughed.

"Are we going to mope, do you think? Life from now on. My dried out husk of art and your chewed up marriage. Sorry, our chewed up marriages, I mean. Look at us. Life, eh? Let's drink to that." Hugh raised his glass but Elise wasn't up for the humor of it. Hugh lowered his hand. "Come on Elise. What does anything matter? Look, Jack's not going to drop you in it. He's not like that, I mean, he feels bad about all this. Guilt will keep him generous. Has he spoken to the children yet?"

"What do *you* think?"

"I'm thinking I want to keep out of things just at the moment. He's out of New York. On break still. The new semester starts this week. He'll be in touch. I'm sorry."

"Don't be."

There was a silence before Elise looked up.

"Did you get in touch with Michael? Don't you want to see him sometime?" She shook her head. "How does that all work?"

Hugh looked lost at the questions. It was his turn to feel uncomfortable.

"I don't know. I've no idea. I think men are different. Dads, I mean. Actually, we talked about Joseph, you know, the carpenter. It's quite funny, when you think of it . . . the whole Christian nonsense. But actually, it was Jonah's point. The boy had obviously really thought about the whole Pieta thing. It got me thinking about absent fathers. Joseph was usurped. Dads get pushed out."

Hugh just came out with it. He knew it was hardly something Elise would want to hear. But he was tired of pussy footing around all the crap.

"So I'm to feel sorry for Jack?"

"Knew you'd say that. Look, there are no victims. You and I are the male-female recipients of our respective spouses' . . . what? Foibles? Personalities. I don't know. I don't see myself as a victim."

"Neither do I. Of course I don't. It's not about us, it's about the innocents. Children. Remember them?"

Hugh frowned.

"Look, don't start saying fathers don't give a shit and it's all down to mums. Marianne was no victim of my vice. God, how I hate this petty blame game! As if accepting or apportioning blame will solve anything. The kids are only victims if we adults teach them how to point fingers. Michael doesn't have to vote on his favorite parent. He thinks we're both shits."

"Oh, I see. I'm a shit too? Like Jack?"

"Oh come on. No. I'm not talking about your situation."

"Well, I am. I'd like to. Well?"

"No. Of course you're not." Hugh looked at her a little guiltily. He sighed. "Okay. I'm sorry. Let's not fight. I concede. You *are* a victim. Yes, of course you are. You didn't deserve any of this. *Me*? I'm not a victim, perhaps. I didn't let myself become one. Like jumping before being pushed. Whatever. So, there you are. Does it feel better – feeling wronged?"

Elise lowered her eyes and shook her head. Hugh felt she was on the brink of tears. He put his hand across the table and reached for hers.

"I'm sorry. I mean . . . yep, it's crap. I know. Life."

"It's not the hurt pride. It's the lack of love. It's gut wrenching. I mean, a family is an attempt to create a private world of trust in a storm and then it just all gets blown to shit and all the bits get scattered and lost. Everything falls apart. What could have been . . . the lie. I still believe in the family. It's not romantic. Hugh? It's not naïve of me. It was a dream and it has all gone. That's what's sad. I'm not a victim of my situation; it's a universal tragedy. Men don't feel it so much. I think women have to live for the dream. We're sort of programmed that way. We can't just walk off. You can . . . and Jack. I can't. My world is broken."

Hugh half listened to the tail end of Elise's words. Something earlier had caught his attention. He was making a connection.

"Wait. I think I have it." Hugh raised his hand and Elise looked at him, raising her eyebrows.

"Have what?"

"The Pieta. You know, these objects, these things . . . what do we call them?"

"I've no idea." Elise's voice was flat. Uninterested.

"Works, sculptures. These things people put together. They're sort of meeting points, forums of minds."

"You're changing the subject. Fair enough. Off me onto you. Maybe I will have something to eat. Do you want another beer?" Elise began to rise.

Hugh looked up at her a little surprised.

"No wait. It *is* about you."

Elise frowned. She hesitated before stepping away from her chair.

"Tell me in a minute. I'll get another round in. And some crisps. What flavor?"

Hugh looked annoyed.

"Oh, anything. Thanks."

Elise left him. He had time to catch up with his thoughts, at least. Or rather, it was an image. All the complexity of what they had been talking about came down to a single image. A misunderstood icon. Jonah was right. These images, the myths were about *us*. Jung and Freud had spent too much time on the Greeks. Why had they ignored the Bible? The Pieta wasn't about a mother's grief for her lost son, the son of God.

It was about the loss of family. Elise had said it all just now. The way everything just fell apart. A broken world. God was life. A sort of pantheistic malign spirit. The storm of a world.

Elise was returning from the bar with new drinks and bags of crisps on a little round tray. She walked carefully, arms out straight so not to spill anything.

"Here. Let me." Hugh got up to help.

"It's okay. I've got it. Sit." Elise smiled at him as she slipped the tray over the top of the table.

"Thanks. I owe you."

"You can get the next round," Elise replied, stepping back around to her chair.

Hugh removed their drinks from the tray.

"So we're up for a lock in?"

"Could be. Well, what's your brainwave? You were saying just now."

"Oh. Yes. It's complicated but basically you're Mary."

"I'm Mary."

Hugh nodded to confirm.

"I haven't worked it out yet. It's not clear in my mind. But the Pieta has something to do with the mother mourning the loss of her family. It's got nothing to do with God or the Messiah. It's mythic. My Pieta must be true to the myth. If the Bible stories didn't have some sort of resonance with our psyches, no one would be bothered with them. I need to perform a sort of circumambulation."

Elise didn't look interested.

• • •

They took the Long Island Rail Road from Oyster Bay to Penn Station midday to avoid the commuter rush. The break had left Jack disorientated and tumbling in free fall which, while he sat looking out at the sidings, the rolling stock passing through Garden City and Hempstead and on westward, he quite liked. Wasn't that what he had come in search of?

Amy had her freckled nose buried in a book. She had class reading to catch up on. He had plenty of time to reflect on the obvious symbolism of their return to Manhattan: life was a journey, blah, blah, blah. The journey now wasn't from Amy's family home empty and abandoned by her professional parents (mother in Washington ostensibly writing a book on state-run media and the crisis in journalism, father in Berne ostensibly at a winter pharmaceuticals convention – who cared?) but from Cornwall.

Wealth or money at least allowed you to get lost, lose frames of reference, and go spinning out of orbit into exquisite space. He had done it. He had lost gravity, and once you slipped away there was no getting back. What had held him now repulsed him. The little blue planet of his life was melting into the blackness and it saddened him a little to see it falling away.

On into the void and recklessly he floated, with no planet to pull him down, but rather, a space-companion who just hung there – no unbalanced forces upon her, no gravitational attraction drawing him. This was the authentic existence: no frames, no places; the unmoved and uninterrupted self suspended. This was Amy's world, the world of a bright free spirit, a spoiled Long Island only child transplanted and unable or disinclined to commit to anything except everything. *Also sprach Zarathustra.*

The train trundled through suburbia on to Queens. Amy lowered her book and looked up. She glanced out at the increasing insistence of the city. She looked back at Jack and smiled. And he smiled too because they were caught in a moment of shy self-consciousness for the first time, like young lovers who suddenly realize they're not two individuals alone anymore but one. And then she frowned and looked away as if someone had just walked over her grave.

18

It was Monday and Jonah needed to see Mrs. Jerwood. He had to make up for lost time and his coursework was so behind. The connection with what Mr. Borne had said over the weekend about the Pieta, and now his own schoolwork, festered in his mind – had done on the walk to school. What force, precisely, was it that reduced the noble pleasure of creative acts to the tedium of work? Jonah knew there was a fundamental problem, not just with his own immediate experience but for all times, all places. People seldom did things because they wanted. Where did necessity come from? Biology? Culture?

"Hey Jonah! Jo. Wait."

The call from a familiar voice interrupted his thoughts. He had nearly reached the school gates. He glanced around and saw Simon Rockshaw putting on some pace to catch up. He was on his own, so that was okay.

"Your mum didn't drop you off today then?" Jonah asked, turning back to walk on. Simon was a little out of breath as he came alongside.

"Just on the corner. She's late, like you."

Jonah ignored the dig.

"So how's it going? You still coming over?"

"I just help out in the studio. Tidy up. Make the coffee."

Simon didn't answer.

"I learn stuff too. When Mr. Borne has time, he tells me things, you know, like for art."

Simon nodded.

"Sure. Look, there's a gig next Saturday. Fancy playing?"

Jonah pretended not to look surprised or pleased even. He shrugged his shoulders nonchalantly enough.

"Dunno. What happened to Weekes?"

"Can't do it. You know it all. There's no new songs or anything. Up to you, anyway. I got to go. I'll miss homeroom."

Simon held onto his school bag and started to jog on. Jonah watched him go.

They were up by the first school buildings and now he didn't have time left to reflect on the implications of what Simon had said. But it kind of knocked him a bit – sort of an unexpected pleasant threat of something. Since having been kicked out of the band, he had come accustomed to the exile and had quite liked it. Now this.

The school bell began to ring; he had missed attendance and the day now took him clumsily in its hands.

• • •

"It will die. The 'we' of 'us' will fade and wither away. We will sense it, feel it shift uneasily to the side of our friendship and then, and then we will part. There is no working at it. There is no holding onto some dying relationship. Vanish, ye phantoms! from my idle spright, into the clouds, and never more return! Does it make you sad? People trap themselves in misery because they would not be sad."

Amy pushed herself up onto her elbow, her head now resting on the heel of her hand, her loose hair ruffled down. Jack caught the lashes of her eyes almost in his imagination as if they had already become a detail of a memory. He was drowsy from sex and the dim light of the bedroom.

"If we're permanently parting, we'll never split. Isn't that the secret?" he asked softly.

Amy leaned forward and rested her head on his chest. She felt the weight of Jack's arm enfold her. His heart beating in her ear.

"The secret of permanence lies in the threat of imminent departure. Change. No . . . yes, it does, actually, but I don't want permanence. I hate the thought of it."

"That's because you're young."

"Young is a state of mind. There are kids younger than me who are older than you."

She felt him inhale deeply. Her head rose on his chest.

"It *is* Keatsian. You're right. I mean, I hadn't realized that floating in space would be endless melancholy. I thought it would be freeze-dried ecstasy."

"Nothing's endless. Keats died."

She felt Jack chuckle silently. It jiggled her head slightly.

"Oh no, he didn't. For starters, he's in bed with us and the rest is stuffed in an urn. Art suspends it all and we cling to it and we grasp the ancient by the collar and stare into his face for affirmation."

"Jack?"

"What?"

"Fucking makes me all poetic."

"Me too."

"Jack?"

"Yes?"

"I don't want ever to love you. But I like the poetry when it comes now and again."

"Sure. Me too."

• • •

"Of course it's a midlife crisis. How dumb we are to stumble into these disasters as if we didn't know they were there just waiting for us . . . not hidden but bloody great elephants. It was there, Hugh, standing in the road a mile away. Staring."

"It's a label. I don't even know what a midlife crisis is. Did *I* have one? Is it something all men are destined to get, like prostate cancer?"

"Yes. Yes it is. And you *did* have a midlife crisis. You all have to fuck a younger woman for some weird pathetic reason as if you couldn't do anything better. I mean, why don't we prepare for it like saving for college fees and pensions?"

Hugh raised his eyebrows and shrugged. He was still wondering if he had had a midlife crisis. It hadn't really occurred to him.

"Do you think that was all it was?"

"What?"

"It sort of belittles one, really. I mean, as if everything we do in life is predetermined by our biology."

"It is. It's all a bloody farce. We're like cats and dogs. We're all just stupid fuckers."

Hugh laughed.

"Well, at least we can see the funny side of it all."

Elise frowned.

"I don't want it to be funny. I want it to be tragic."

"One more?"

There were already six empty glasses on the table between them. Elise nodded. She looked at him.

"Okay. One."

Hugh got up a little carefully and looked toward the bar, now quite busy.

"And you can tell me what it's like having a midlife crisis. What it feels like from the inside," she called just before he drifted off.

When he got to the bar, he felt local eyes upon him. He fished around in his pockets for money as a distraction. The barman came over and, somehow, Hugh felt conversations around him resume.

"I'll have a pint of the dry cider. No, actually. Make that two. Thanks."

"Jack Rockshaw not back yet? Still away?" came a voice from Hugh's right.

Hugh looked up. The name sounded so familiar. It didn't occur to him, immediately, that he was being addressed.

"Not back for Christmas?"

Hugh looked more carefully.

"I'm sorry. I didn't realize. Um, Jack? You know Jack?"

There was a bearded guy next to him wearing a dark blue fisherman's smock.

"Sorry mate. I'm in your way."

With that, the man stepped back. Hugh could now see the person who had spoken. He was round faced. Bald. Sitting on a stool at the end of the bar.

"John Davies. I know Simon. Help out with the band now and again."

Hugh nodded and pretended to have perhaps heard of him through Simon.

"Nice to meet you. Yes, Simon's band. They're getting quite a few gigs."

"Two ciders," came the barman's voice.

"Oh. That's me. Thanks."

"That's £4.90."

"There's five. Keep it. Thanks. Um, Jack Rockshaw. No, he's in New York. It was just all too much, I think. He's got quite a big exhibition coming up."

Hugh was keen to get going. He felt the man's eyes on him. There was something searching and judgmental.

"Right. Last one for the road," he said rather inanely.

The man nodded. He said nothing.

Hugh lifted the glasses off the bar and turned to leave. He caught the man glancing round at their table by the window. Elise was looking out into the darkening day, elbows resting amongst the empty glasses and her head nestled in her hands. Hugh was glad to leave and walked purposefully away.

"The Dark Monarch snoops in Cuckoo Town still, I see," Hugh announced, placing the drinks on the table and nudging the empty glasses along.

Elise looked round from the window.

"Thanks."

Hugh sat down.

"Don't look, but the man at the bar . . . John Davies. Know him?"

Elise nodded and lifted her pint off the table. She glanced over.

"Oh yes. John. He's Justin's dad. He helps out with some of the gigs. Has to really. Justin's the drummer."

"Oh. I see. Well, he's curious, I'd say. Mind you, it's fair enough. I mean, Jack not back for Christmas and this strange man now hanging around. The chorus really does exist. Coryphaeus seems most intrigued."

Elise lowered her glass and smiled.

"I should put my tongue in your ear. See if he chokes on his beer."

Hugh smiled back. He was glad to see a glimmer of the old Elise. It made him wonder at how they had aged.

"Did your dad ever have an affair, other women?" he asked.

Elise raised her eyebrows and leaned back.

"Well, not that I knew of. But he would have. People were more discrete when divorce wasn't as fashionable as it is now. No one feels obliged to keep up the pretense anymore. I suppose it must be better in some ways. Better for women, though I'm not so sure . . . What about you?"

Hugh frowned and leaned his elbows on the edge of the table. He stared at his cider.

"Same, really. I mean the pretense. But I think my mother might have strayed. Oddly. She liked a party and my father was really rather a bore."

"So you got your libido from your mother then."

Hugh looked up.

"Do you think I'm over libidinous?"

"Marianne wasn't enough."

Hugh narrowed his eyes at Elise's provocation. He decided to let the comment pass. Must be the booze.

"Of course, our parents tiptoed in and out of bedrooms and kept things going for the children's sake. They were selfish, but only up to a point. That's all changed now."

Hugh wasn't sure where Elise was taking the conversation. She was planting some digs at him.

"You think I was selfish? Maybe a little narcissistic?" he asked.

Elise studied him and shrugged.

"I don't think you're narcissistic. Funnily enough I always think it's women who are vain in that self-absorbed way. And gays, of course. It's rather camp to be staring at yourself all day. You know, glancing at yourself in shop windows. Selfish?" She shook her head. It was kind of her. "No, I don't think of you that way either. Okay, I'm not trying to make a parallel between us. Jack isn't you and I'm certainly not Marianne. She was a cold hard bitch. I never understood why you married her. She wasn't even that well connected."

Hugh laughed gently at the throwaway remarks. The suggestions. Elise could be a spiteful wit when she wanted. Hugh decided to parry.

"And you've never felt the urge to stray?"

Elise was ready for the question. It was almost as if she'd set him up. She shook her head.

"Kids, Hugh. If mothers had nannies, they'd be fucking away like rabbits, I'm sure. Oh, to be rich. It must be wonderful."

"You're joking. So, you would if you could? Have you thought about it? Do you have fantasies?"

"Of course I do. Even the queen masturbates."

Hugh nodded and laughed again.

"So, the whole sex thing comes down to the Ring of Gyges, the fear of getting caught. The only difference between the sex-starved spouse and the adulterer is that one is scared, the other reckless. So much for the moral high ground."

"Or that one puts others' needs above their own."

"Then to hell with it all! Children only get upset if they're told by society to be upset. Stupid, fucking religion again."

Hugh felt the fourth cider beginning to play with him. He lowered his voice. He didn't want to fall into a drunken argument with Elise. It was the last thing he wanted. He tried to correct his position. He leaned forward, almost halfway across the table. His elbow nudged an empty glass.

"Can't we tell our children that marriage isn't sacred, that it's perfectly reasonable to be polygamous? Did I sign up for the bill of monogamy as soon as I was born? I didn't ask to be born a Muslim or a Christian. A Jew. I'm not any of these. But all that crap has been dumped on us. And I'm sick that I allowed the social mores to be passed onto Michael, who will pass it on in his miserable turn to extend the chain of victims far into future generations of needlessly ruined lives."

"Amen." Elise raised her glass for a toast. Hugh glanced at her a little uncertainly. "Here's to swingers!"

Hugh looked at his own glass and rose to the irony with drunken defiance. He grasped at his glass.

"Yes. Here's to swingers and gang bangs!"

"Ménages à trois!"

"Orgies!"

"Porn!"

"Donkeys!"

19

When Elise saw Jack's pale, drawn face appear on her laptop, it occurred to her that, perhaps he was ill. Not physically ill but that he was having a nervous breakdown. And then, in the continuing moment's silence, she began to wonder if this whole affair was just an elaborate symptom of mental collapse. She remembered that Hugh had not gotten around to telling her what it felt like to have a midlife crisis.

Jack spoke first, across what felt like a lifetime apart.

"Elise? Hi."

"Hello Jack."

"I'm glad we can talk. It's not ideal . . ."

"All I have to do is listen. So, I'm listening."

Jack sighed and looked mournful enough.

"Okay. What do you want me to say?"

"Anything. Talk about the weather if you can't talk about anything else. It's a start."

"I'm –"

"But don't say you're sorry."

"I wasn't going to."

It was a bad second step forward. Jack was looking down as if psyching himself up to start again.

"How are the kids?"

"They're fine. They don't know and they're not that interested. They're teenagers."

"Sure. Well, look, first thing I need to say is that I don't want everything to fall apart."

"Jack, it has fallen apart. You want a divorce. I'm redundant."

Jack shook his head.

"Can we have an unscripted conversation? We're both saying the inevitable things people say to each other in this situation. You probably want to know who she is but you won't ask."

"Okay, so who is she? Is she legal?"

Jack gave an exasperated sigh.

"I don't want the house and everything to be split up. There's no need. Look, I'm not attached to this girl. It's not anything like that. We're not in love. We will part company sooner or later. In weeks, maybe."

"It's called a fling."

"It's not called anything, Elise. Okay?"

"It's a midlife crisis. Okay, so get your final fucks in and come home to mummy."

"Right. You're not in the mood. This isn't going to work. But listen, when she and I are done, I'm not coming back."

"Jack?"

"What?"

"Are you depressed? Are you well?"

"I don't know. I'll call back tomorrow. We've made a start. Let it stew for a bit."

"Okay."

"Look . . . Bye."

"Goodnight Jack. Jack –?"

• • •

"Thanks."

Hugh took his coffee from Jonah at the barn door. He'd gone to step outside and he met Jonah on the path. It was a dank, sallow day: quilted silver clouds draped over the sea. Jonah was back at school so now only came on the weekend. Hugh had missed him and was keen to strike up a conversation.

"Can I ask you something personal?"

Jonah looked back a little surprised, maybe a little wary too.

"Okay."

"Do you miss your father?"

There was a long pause. Hugh was about to help by changing the subject or apologizing. But Jonah spoke, looking out over the sea.

"I don't know. I think about him sort of. I mean, every day he's somewhere in my mind. Like he visits just briefly to say hello, you know in my head, and then he goes. Sometimes, usually in the morning when I get up."

Hugh nodded.

"Sure. You're not angry at him?"

Jonah frowned and shook his head.

"How can you be angry at someone who's gone?"

"I don't know. I don't know what happened. It's none of my business. I just wondered. You talked about Joseph the other day. And, well, Elise said you were living with just your mother."

"Oh."

"I'm sorry."

"It doesn't matter."

"It's just that, well, I sort of lost my son. So, we have something in common. In a way . . . "

Jonah nodded and sipped his coffee. He shivered and looked back at the barn.

"I'm getting cold. Can I go in?"

"Yes, of course. I'm sorry. I'll come now." Hugh let the boy leave him. Perhaps he had been too abrupt. Too familiar. Jonah left him standing there looking out at the wide horizon.

• • •

It was the first class of the new semester. Jack didn't feel he'd prepared that well. In England, you could get away with winging it. These students weren't so liberal; they didn't like the ad-lib, the banter, and he hadn't gotten to know their names or even their faces. It depressed him: the iPods, the iPhones, the iPads, the iEyes searching, and iThumbs squirreling away for what? iEnlightenment? An iSoul? And it was for him, now, as the class settled, to plead for their attention followed by an on-screen entertainment of lost memories and a lost world. He felt immediately resentful: thwarted and rather like a dinosaur. Fuck the notes. He decided to speak out.

"Why are we here? Why are you here? What are we all trying to achieve? Okay, that's not a rhetorical question, not a virtual question; it's a straight, upfront, genuine, what-the-fuck-are-we-doing? question and I want all of you to switch off your phones – which you should have done before entering class anyway – and write down your honest answers. And then you're going to read what you've written. If I don't understand or if I don't think they're good reasons, I'll quit wasting any more of my time and there's the door waiting for my potentially imminent departure and I'll get a cab to JFK and then take a plane to Patagonia. Thank you, ladies and gentlemen. You've got five minutes."

The ensuing silence wasn't stunned – they were too life-numb to be stunned – but there was, at least, a sort of reflexive 'uh?' in the air. There were a few head nods, outweighed by a communal mild irritation at the prospect of having to engage with something.

Jack clocked the response. Thirty seconds had elapsed. He had four and a half minutes of his career left and that time to reflect on why he shouldn't just walk out of his life. He wondered, then, if he was perhaps just being competitive with Amy. He wanted to pull the plug before her. Rock-paper-scissors. That was true. But it wasn't so much the challenge as the authenticity. It mattered to him that, when he was gone, she would love him for being true. And that was enough to carry him through the rest of his life. He didn't consider himself ever to have sought self-meaning through others, but Amy was different. Her good opinion of him mattered and he felt defined by her. And then he started to think about Elise –

"Mr. Rockshaw? Sir, may I read my answer out?"

Jack looked up.

"We're done?" he asked. "Okay. I'm ready. Let's do this."

• • •

"No, I think the whole YBA thing has been overdone. It's difficult. How soon can you pull away from trying to wake people up? Maybe we never should. But it's not what I do. There are enough egos out there. Actually, I hate it. Two things kill creativity: money and ego."

Hugh tapped and drew his chisel point skillfully across the granite as he spoke. Jonah watched from behind. He shielded his eyes from flying stone chips.

"Like Sven Berlin," Jonah suggested.

"Maybe. It's hard for an artist to have humility. Everyone's playing convention to change convention. It's also more of a West thing. You don't get it so much in the East."

"Sure."

"See this. Another Pieta. What am I doing? I don't know. If I were Damien Hirst, I'd approach the whole thing differently. It's all down to personality. But in trying to undermine tradition, he creates his own convention. With Hirst, he's even proud of the trademarks. If he were a real rebel, he'd paint a Constable. Trouble is, he can't paint. He's a con artist. A lot of them are. That, or lazy. It came with Thatcherism. The Saatchi brothers. Bank vaults for galleries. There. Think that's done. Need to give my hands a break."

Hugh was half talking to himself. He lowered his mallet and chisel and stepped back from the stone. He glanced at Jonah, who was looking at the emerging work.

"And you've been forced to do it this way," he said, keeping his eyes firmly on the sculpture.

Hugh followed his gaze.

"And how would you have brought yourself to this? How would you break the monotony?"

Jonah frowned and looked thoughtful for a minute.

"I'd have laid them down. Like lying down, side by side. Like lovers. I'd smash the Madonna and child, the upright. The phallocentric thing. The form is wrong. It's dead."

Hugh was intrigued. It was a good answer.

"It's maybe fixed by the *stabat mater dolorosa speciosa* tradition. I don't know why Mary has to be standing. I'm too ignorant of the religious iconography. I'd imagine a good Catholic would know what it all meant. Actually, I did feel that the whole Pieta tradition was more about the loss of a family than of the son of God. That's a more secular view, I suppose."

"Like Lear, you mean?"

"Lear?"

"*King Lear.* I'm doing it at school. It's a set text."

"Oh right. Yes. That's a good comparison. I never thought. You mean Lear is Mary, Cordelia is Christ."

"The absent queen is Joseph."

"Yes. Shakespeare's family life was falling apart. His son had died. His wife was effectively estranged. It's the same sort of myth."

Hugh looked back at his emerging work. He laughed gently to himself.

"What's so funny?" asked Jonah.

"*That.*"

They both looked at the scarred rock. Hugh pointed his chisel at it.

"It's piss poor. That's the trouble with commissions. When it doesn't come from your own genius, you end up knocking something up that could have been so much better. It's all too late. It's not like a painting. I'm stuck with it."

"*They'll* like it."

"And that's my failure. Fucking hell."

Jonah shifted uneasily.

"It's not too late. You can still improvise. Turn it."

Hugh stepped toward the stone, his hands hung low and tired. He started to walk around it like a boxer eyeing up his opponent.

"You know, my trouble is I fall too much in love with the material. I love the stone and deep down all I am is a butcher."

• • •

Gail Singleton, Jonah's mother, sat at the back of the church during Mass. She could hear the traffic in the high street. A seagull beyond.

She closed her eyes and drifted while the half dozen or so in front rose from the pews and shuffled forward to take Communion. How had she let herself sin so? There was nothing left to grasp. Before, there had been something to hold her, but now she had lost all reference. She couldn't even tell how fast she was falling or in which direction. She was shut out – unworthy to take Mass – racing through space in a state of immeasurable stillness. For Mrs. Singleton, there was no freeze-dried ecstasy, no endless sweet melancholy, just an unspeakable loneliness.

20

Hugh had to go back to the moors. He had been wanting to return to the Nine Sisters because all that was contemporary seemed to be breaking apart. The Pieta felt almost like a ruin, Elise had found herself on an empty stage, there was Jonah who haunted him, and on top of it all, he had received a text message from Kate last night. It had read: *Sorry. I miss you. How are you?* The text caused a confusion of irritation, mainly because when his phone rang, he had so hoped it might be Michael and it was always like that and it was never him. We value those who don't miss us more than those who do. But before they had split, Kate had agreed they should move on. They should find new partners, new lives that weren't defined by the car wreck of his marriage. When a man divorces, he leaves *two* women behind. Kate was collateral damage.

So, Hugh hoped to realign himself, banish the quotidian clutter, and reestablish his place within the universal framework.

The autumn browns of his last visit had been leached out to grays and black by the winter. What had been dying was dead and the cold wind snapped. It was a bleak place with pockets of frost in the hollows and strings of spiders' pearls draped along the fallen walls. Had D.H. Lawrence been here? Of course he had. That sensual crust of the earth and the musty soil were there. He had smelled them in the pages. *They had known the intercourse between heaven and earth.* What a wonderful and terrifying man Lawrence must have been. So lost out here in those dark years of the war.

Hugh had reached the stone circle but from the track that led directly up from the road. He had wanted to avoid the Mên-an-Tol and the memories. He wanted to reconnect not to the past as much as to all time. The couch grass bleached by the gray winter skies was firmer underfoot. The soil was thin over the rock. Hugh walked on to the center of the circle, looked around, and he was struck by how much had changed on the surface of things. Three months felt like the passing of his whole life. How might he succeed in taking it all in? For Jonah and Michael, life was where they lived. But for him, at his age, too much of life was elsewhere, on the horizon and in the attics of the mind. The universe was expanding and all that mattered was steadily drifting away. The moon was shrinking off like a thief.

What was the artist to do but shore up the breach and seek to stem the tide of irreversible decline? God, he missed London: talking in the pub and the narrow view. True, he had come here to find the mournful reality of this place and the winter but even Zarathustra had had enough of the mountain solitude after ten years. To seek solitude for answers was futile. There was no meaning out here and beyond. Far better to sit by the fire in Hrothgar's hall and listen to the stories than wander the heath all bad tempered and murderous.

• • •

"I will miss you. Do you think we'll make it to Easter? Do you think you'll be waving goodbye to me at Departures?" Jack studied Amy's face for the real answer before she replied. Amy lifted her cappuccino and took such a feminine sip, lip on lip and then, when she lowered her cup again, Jack saw the little bead of foam along the fine line between her skin and sensuality. She glanced down against his infatuation, a little self-conscious, a little annoyed.

"You're in love, Mr. Rockshaw," she said behind downcast eyelashes, a freckled nose, and the sheen of her hair.

"It's not like you to be demure," he replied.

She looked up and smiled with quick blue eyes.

"What a lovely word. Is that an English word, do you think? I've never heard someone say that here." Suddenly she mocked a serious, thoughtful frown. "Does it come from the French do you think? For 'wall'?"

Jack was happy enough to let the conversation turn away from her.

"Don't feel it. I mean, it doesn't make sense. Well, I don't know. Maybe a wall is sort of a defense. Modesty? Hmm. Don't know."

"Oh Jack. We'll have such sweet sorrow. It's lovely, like life is just a slow departure. Think how many lives we have left to live. Do you think 'love' and 'live' are related?"

Jack was suddenly not in the mood for Amy's jokes. They always bordered on ridicule when he just wanted her to cheer him up with something closer to affection than it was.

"Will you ever love someone, Amy? Will you ever dare to live love?"

"That's hyphenated, right?"

Jack shook his head.

"It's a verb, then a noun."

"I don't know. Seriously. Maybe I should be worried I'm such a love skeptic. I have such deep problems with words. Maybe I will only ever love in retrospect. I don't see why unrequited love has to be prospective. Better to have lost and loved than never to have lost at all."

"You've lost me."

"I love it."

"You are too smart, young lady."

They smiled at each.

"Oh Jack, I'm feeling too horny for a public place. Anyway, I've told you, I lust you. That's a verb, not a noun, and that's how it is. Love should be a physical thing. An action. A behavior. I hate the idea of it being just a state of mind like piety. Maybe it's my psychology major or my atheism. Maybe it's just that. Little things in a young life are pretty damn influential. You know, mister, you got to be careful with me. I'm highly tuned and fragile and I'm laying down my life here. Whatever you say or do to me could cause irreparable damage. Like if you fucked my ass without affection, I might never overcome my kleptomania come my mid-forties." She shrugged. "Who knows. We have asymmetry here. You and I."

• • •

Elise was checking the orders that had arrived. The boxes were stacked along the wall, since there was no room at the back of the shop. She must sort out her stock this spring. Maybe spend a Sunday clearing stuff out. There were loads of samples she could ditch. Clear out the back cupboards and shelves. The frames from Denmark hadn't arrived. She desperately needed the ash frames for Mrs. Haffod's three canvasses. Two weeks now . . .

In spite of the little stresses and frustrations, it was good to be away from the house and working at the shop. Work distracted her. Last night, Jack had sent an e-mail about future plans. He thought he would visit after his contract in New York came to an end. He didn't expect to stay on in the States. It would be an upheaval. He really was just throwing his life up in the air. Elise hoped he would leave and make a mess of things; it would make what he had been doing seem a little more authentic at least and she might like him more for that. It would allow her to feel concerned about him and to worry from a distance – watch the fall. She didn't feel vengeful, it was more of a maternal thing: a premonition of how she would have to cope when Simon and Caja left the nest.

How would she cope with motherhood with no one to mother? Perhaps she could start an animal sanctuary. Or a sanctuary for lost men. She already had two. One definitely. She let her mind drift. There wasn't much else to do. She smiled at the thought that Hugh and Jack and now Jonah were just stray cats wondering in and out for a little food, a little warmth now and then. She didn't want dogs because they were too loyal and got protective. There was more honesty in cats, somehow, in the way they came back but really didn't give a shit like they never could quite work out who you were; cat lovers were always rather anonymous in Cat World.

But that would all be very agreeable, she decided, to live the second half of her life as a provider of protection and free of possessiveness and control. Perhaps Jack was right to be cracking up like this. After all, what were they hanging onto other than a false sense of security and a stifling world. Wasn't he freeing her too? Once Simon and Caja were off, she was free. She could sell the house, the shop, take the money, and run.

The thought pleased her. She lowered the order list in her hand and looked down at the boxes, a glint of contempt in her eyes.

"Right. That's done. Wonder if I should phone Denmark," she said aloud. She spoke to herself a lot these days. Maybe she should be more aware of it.

It was wet out: a fine squally, misty rain almost like smoke. The postman was making his deliveries. He wore shorts even in the winter. Perhaps he preferred wet skin to wet trousers. It would be more comfortable, and walking up and down the steep streets of St. Ives must keep him pretty warm and then he'd be out surfing in the afternoon. What a waterlogged, water-filled, watery life. Indoors would be uncomfortable. The thought made her shudder.

She was just looking out at the rain, the street, the infrequent passerby, and a life hemmed in. No customers this time of the year. She missed the visitors, the tourists in this winter fallow time.

With almost a sigh, she turned away, but not before she caught, in the corner of her eye, Jonah's mother walking past. Her heart froze whenever she saw Mrs. Singleton. Elise stopped herself and watched with a frown. She desperately wanted to reach out, ask her in for a cup of coffee, have a little gossip, talk about the town. Mrs. Singleton walked on and seemed to float away like she had already died.

• • •

"But it's not art is it."

Mrs. Jerwood smiled. She looked down at the card in her hands as she invited the class to comment. She had a small wedge of the cards on her desk. She picked up another.

"What about this one?" she asked.

"Oh, I love that. Who's it by, Miss?"

"Anyone know?"

Jonah raised his hand.

"It's Jack Vettriano. The Laughing Butler or something."

Mrs. Jerwood nodded.

"Well done. It's *The Singing Butler* by Jack Vettriano. Art?"

"No, Miss."

"Okay. Why not?"

"It's just a postcard. It's too commercial."

Mrs. Jerwood smiled. She looked at Jonah.

"What do you think of it, Jonah?"

Jonah looked up and thought before he spoke.

"I like it for what you *can't* see. But it's silly."

Mrs. Jerwood turned the picture round in her hand and looked at it. She smiled and held it back up for the class.

"So what can you see that is invisible?"

Jonah spoke for the class because it was his perception and he wanted to go on.

"The wind. And the characters sort of work in a way but it's the intention. It's nostalgic, escapist crap. Sentimental. That's why idiots buy it. But it should be sinister and upsetting. It could be sort of edgy but it isn't. It's a soppy birthday card. And anyway, the dancers don't look right and it's lazy realism. People love this sort of stuff because it's easy and simple-minded and they're simple-minded and it's depressing, really."

"Oh right, Jonah. So I suppose you'd prefer dead sharks and unmade beds," said Caja.

Jonah turned and looked at Simon's sister. He felt oddly hurt. Caja was having a go at him and she never normally said a thing in class – just would sit there sulking and sour-faced. Jonah turned back to look at Mrs. Jerwood. He addressed her, not Caja.

"No. They're both frauds after money. The one tries to be popular and easy, the other tries to shock. One is Saturday night TV, the other is porn. Real artists don't give a crap who's going to buy anything. It's not about chasing money. You can see the greed as easily as the honesty and you never get the two together."

JESUS THE HOMELESS,
© TIM SCHMALZ, 2011

FEBRUARY

21

February brought snow. It sprinkled the moors of Cornwall with cold white dust and it laid a blanket over Manhattan's streets and sidewalks during the night and it melted on the Atlantic waves like icing sugar. And winter said, I am here and I remain.

• • •

"Shall I close the door?" Jonah asked, standing with their coffees, framed against the snow-flecked sky and the garden. Hugh's fingers were numb, his hands mottled with slightly worrying purple and blue. It was as if they were a sign that the stone was beating him. Every hammer blow seemed to take a chip out of his being. He folded his arms, tucking his hands into his armpits.

"You're cold," he affirmed.

"Not as cold as you," Jonah replied.

Hugh nodded and shivered. He shook his head as if in disbelief.

"I knew this was going to kill me."

Jonah closed the door with his foot and the clatter echoed slightly. He brought the steaming coffees over, raising the one toward Hugh as he got close.

"No. I can't. Put it on there." Hugh nodded at the table. "My hands. My fingers are shot."

Jonah frowned with concern but said nothing. He did as he was told.

"What I hate about sculpture is that the disaster unfolds so slowly. It's like the hour hand of a clock. But so much time is chiseled into it just to be dismissed, when finished, with no more than a blink. There's no art in work.

Jonah listened but he watched the hewn rock as if its forms were even now emerging. There were two figures, though rough and incomplete, a saddle pass between their shoulders, great cliff faces, and glacial scree below.

"You know that film *American Beauty* by Sam Mendes?" asked Jonah.

Hugh shivered a nod.

"It started as a whodunit and they changed it on the way."

Hugh shook his head.

"You can't do that with stone. I'm not a director. You can't edit stone. It's the least plastic of the arts. Look what it's doing to me. Go and touch it if you want. See how hard it is."

Jonah looked at the sculpture and stepped closer and a little round to catch an angle. Hugh watched him.

"What do *I* know?" the boy said after a while. He looked down. "I don't understand. Do you *need* the money?"

"As a matter of fact, I do."

"Then it was never going to be good, was it."

"No. And it's ripping my tendons. My fingers are banana bunches." Hugh laughed and stepped toward the table for his coffee.

"I couldn't do it. I mean, make something because I had to, you know, for money," said Jonah.

Hugh nodded and reached carefully for his mug with both hands.

"Well, it's also a penance." He sniffed and turned to look at his work face on. "I'm here to atone for the sins of the father."

Hugh looked at Jonah who looked back and smiled.

• • •

"How many succeed in pushing the horizon out beyond themselves? How many human beings ever manage to decenter? All you ever witness is the screaming importance of the self. And it bores the shit out of me. I think it's got a lot to do with consumer culture don't you?"

"It's still snowing."

Jack let the curtain fall back and moved from the window. There was a pillar of gray light now where the drapes didn't meet. He ignored it and turned to look at Amy on the bed.

"You're restless. How can you be restless at this time of year?" she asked.

Jack frowned, still reluctant to move from where he stood. He felt a little numb.

"I need something. I need lifting up."

"We all do. Everyone's living in a well."

Jack liked the image because it was silly. He smiled.

"Life is snow. It just keeps falling. And every time you plough it away, more falls overnight. That's what work is. It's shoveling drifts."

"I can see your cock."

Jack glanced down. His dressing gown had chosen to mimic the curtains. He laughed and pulled it wide open baring all.

"Oh Mr. Rockshaw, your semi is screaming at me."

Jack looked down again.

"More of a shout, really."

Amy parked the page in her book and closed it. She placed it down on the pillow beside her.

"Okay. So let's get drunk and fuck all day."

"I want to go out," said Jack, glancing at the drapes.

"Where to? It's snowing. It's Sunday. It goes back to when you were a kid. You want to go out and make a snowman."

Jack tugged his robe together. He was getting cold. He walked back to the bed.

"How did you get to be so smart?" Jack moved the book and lay down beside her. "Gertrude Stein. Any good?"

"Books are beginning to tire me. At least she doesn't scream. More a sort of grunting yelp, like maybe she's being porked by Picasso."

"Amy, I do believe everything comes down to sex with you." Jack pulled at the duvet covers and looked up at her. Amy looked down at him.

"It's a perspective. Sex perception." She shrugged. "Freud started it. Don't blame me." She wriggled herself down and their faces met. Their arms reached out to each other.

"Oh, your hand's really cold."

"Your hip's really warm. And your thigh." He pulled their bodies together like the closing of a clam.

• • •

"Without the obscurity and the loneliness of it all, artists would cease to be heroes."

"Thanks." Hugh put his empty mug on the table. His mind was on the pain and the chisel. He wasn't really listening. He sensed Jonah moving away.

"Shall I open the door?"

"Eh?"

"The door. Do you want it open again?"

"No. I don't want you getting ill. Anyway, it's *my* penance not yours. What were you saying?"

Jonah hovered over by the door. Hugh peeped round the Pieta to see him. The boy approached.

"Just a thought I had. I mean, we had a discussion last week in class about, you know, what is art? And I was thinking about what we were talking about last weekend. I think art only exists when it's being made. It's like a flower. Once picked, it starts to die."

Hugh rested the point of his chisel on a ridge of stone.

"Ah well, maybe you're right. Maybe all art is a performance. It's good to think of it that way. The audience turns up when the gig's over. That's funny. I like the irony. Sure. Here, you'd better step back." Hugh lifted the point and the mallet. He thought and then spoke as he tapped away.

"You know, maybe all works of art should only be allowed to exist for a limited time. Everything. Even books. Maybe while the person who created it is alive. It should then be buried, you know, put in the grave. It's all just hoarding. There's this anxiety that, suddenly, humans aren't going to be able to say what they've been saying for thousands of years."

"Burn down the Louvre."

"Why not? It's all just packratting in the final analysis."

"Shall I sweep?"

"Sure. Just mind your eyes. You know, I ought to get you involved more. Maybe teach you how to chip rock. Maybe even let you have a go. Perhaps I should do that."

Jonah had brought the broom back from where it had been leaning against the wall. He started to sweep around the back of the plinth.

"Really? I'm learning a lot just being here. I watch. I like to talk."

"Sure. But I know you better. Maybe you'll be a great artist one day and people will find out I only ever let you make coffee. What a legacy! Apparently Hepworth was a complete bitch to her assistants?"

"Was she?"

"Oh yes. She used to hide them away in cupboards when buyers came around. One of them was hidden so long, he pissed his pants. It trickled down the garden path right down to her feet. So I've heard."

"Why was she so hard?"

"Art makes you hard. I don't know. She was ambitious and a woman in traditionally a man's craft. Maybe she was just a bitch. I think fame maybe got the better of her. The pleasanter artists get discovered after they're dead."

• • •

"So when's dad get back?" asked Caja.

Their daughter, Caja, occasionally emerged from her room and would hang about for half an hour or so and grab at something to eat before disappearing again. She spoke in brief extracts that would surface somehow from the dark privacy of her mind. They were all Elise had to go on. Sometimes she would marvel at what had happened to her bubbly, inquisitive child. But more recently, she just felt tired. Faintly bored and driven away. She hovered behind the sofa and looked over. There was a computer game on the flat screen TV: rotating icons, looped animation of men running through bombed out buildings. A gun sight. There was a plate with half a sandwich balanced on the arm of the couch.

"Don't you find that depressing? No homework?"

"It's Sunday, Mum."

"Oh. Well, anyway, your father should be back in three weeks."

There was no reply. The sight moved onto a target and there was the muffled sound of gunfire.

"Where's Simon?"

"Dunno. Upstairs."

"Well, could you tell him to bring down his school clothes? I'm doing a big wash. Caja? Did you hear me?"

"Yes. *All right*."

Elise narrowed her eyes and was about to reply. She decided not to, but took her anger away back to the kitchen.

She was lost in herself when the back door opened and Hugh came in from the porch. She was sorting the clothes on the floor in front of the washing machine.

"Oh, hello. Busy?" came Hugh's voice. It irritated her slightly.

"Only gods have rest days."

"Can I do anything?"

Elise laughed outright and then looked up. He was hovering not far from the door. He looked a little awkward and was staring at her. She straightened herself up and sighed.

"Yes. You can pour me a glass of fucking wine."

Hugh smiled.

"I see."

"I'll have some of that on the table. It's already open."

"Sure. Come and talk to me." Hugh moved to the table and pulled out a chair.

"Okay. Tell me the mystery of the teenager. Where does all the hate come from?" she asked.

"Oh, Caja?" Hugh asked as he sat down. He had taken the bottle and was pouring. Elise went and joined him.

"Well?"

Hugh handed her a full glass.

"Place," he said.

Elise frowned.

"Maybe ten percent is hormones. The rest is environmental. A lot comes from school. The system. And, of course, there's the whole power dynamic thing."

"Oh."

"You sound disappointed."

"I thought it might be something far more exciting and extreme, like insanity or some kind of hardwired evil."

"In a way it is. The madness and the evil are in the culture." Hugh leaned back and sipped his wine. His chair creaked. "I reckon if you took Caja to, I don't know, somewhere like Rajasthan, she'd be transformed in a week. You'd see your daughter again."

Elise felt suddenly tearful. Hugh was right. There was a bright, healthy girl in there. It was as if she had been possessed. Oddly, just then, she thought of Jack. She lowered her glass.

"Is that why Jack is running away? It is, isn't it? He's fleeing to save himself from this nightmare. This fucking house. This life."

Hugh looked subdued.

"Maybe. I don't know."

"So what can I do? Throw it all up in the air? Perhaps I should."

"You can't. You're trapped. If you were rich, maybe you'd be able to sail around the world for a year. Homeschool your kids. All that. The only thing that might shift you otherwise would be a war or a catastrophe, like a famine. Something that would knock the whole thing down. But it's all too big otherwise for any individual to reject. You know, if you look at what people did during the last war, the refugees from Europe all heading off to America, starting from scratch and working their way up again, a lot of them did pretty well. The ones who stayed behind ended up in the ghettoes and the camps. What you need is an incendiary bomb land on your house. Fuck it all up. I mean, like when you're out somewhere. Shopping, say."

"That's funny."

Hugh leaned forward, suddenly rather earnest. He turned his glass by the stem.

"We're lazy. Homo sapiens *domesticus.* We've been tamed in captivity for so long we let others shove us onto cattle trucks. That's how weak we have become. And every government knows that. The whole of Britain has been turned into one big cul-de-sac. If we weren't so weak and suburbanized, we'd all be running for the hills screaming. Yes, that's what we should be doing and maybe that's what Jack has seen."

Elise sighed.

"I hope not. That might make him rather attractive and I want him to be just a twat."

22

Hugh was desperate to talk to Jack. Something about the day had left him feeling like he was waking up, resurfacing. There are triggers in the brain that bring us from sleep to consciousness. The night fades and time shakes us with another day. Hugh hoped Jack would be in. It was a Sunday evening after all. Work tomorrow.

He switched the light on in his studio bedsit. He closed the door on the dark cold outside and went to turn on the small heater by the desk. Then he sat down and picked up his iPad. He opened the screen and scrolled through for FaceTime.

You there? He wrote.

Almost immediately, there was a reply.

Hi Hugh.

Can we talk?

Sure, came the response.

In a second Jack was calling and his pixelated face bubbled onto the screen.

"Hi."

"Hello Jack. Can we talk?"

"How are things? How's Elise? I sent her an e-mail on Friday."

"She's good enough. Actually, she's taking things pretty well."

"Really?"

"I mean she's not going to pieces. You're coming back, right?"

Jack nodded. He was distant.

"Yes. I don't think the exhibition will extend. I'll wrap things up here in three weeks." He looked up and gave a wry smile. "Face the music, Hugh. Is that right? Is that what you want to talk about?"

"What are you going to do? I mean in the long term?"

Jack sighed.

"I don't know. You did it. You got out. What are *you* going to do? Tell me. What's it like being on the other side? Are you free? You've landed on your feet, haven't you?"

"I'm not trying to suggest anything, Jack. You do what you like. I don't have the guilt you're likely to face."

"Don't say Elise doesn't deserve this."

"She doesn't. Look, anyway, it's not about just desserts. It's about what it is you're trying to achieve."

"How's the Pieta?"

"It's shit."

"Tell me about it. I mean, tell me how it is. What's wrong?"

Hugh was happy enough to let Jack change the subject. In some ways, he wanted to off-load his own woes to a friend. Maybe he could set an example for Jack.

"My heart's just not in it. I tried. I really tried to get into this one. But you know how it is. Elise was so encouraging. I think she's more disappointed than I am. They'll be happy enough with whatever crap I come up with. No one knows what's good or bad anymore. No one cares."

"Sure."

"How about you? All lined up I bet."

Jack smiled.

"I've added a couple. You know, the nudes. Amy looks stunning. I'll send you copies if you like."

Hugh didn't know what to say. He didn't want to come across all prudish and priggish so he kept with it.

"What will Amy do? So you're leaving her."

"It's not a fling. It has no label, Hugh. This has been a moment in my life. Something I'll cherish."

"And you can't come back from all that? I'm sure Elise would be fine."

Jack shook his head.

"It's not about Elise. It's not about Amy. Do you think my life revolves around women? Does yours? Are we slaves to our dicks? Come on Hugh, you know this isn't about pussy. It's about freedom. We use women to liberate ourselves. That's our intention, at least."

Hugh laughed.

"Yeah, well, they're the last things we should be running after for that."

Jack shook his head.

"No. Don't be so sure. I got just what I wanted from Amy. She's a genuine free spirit."

"Oh, I see. This is about kids, family, mortgage. Responsibility. Duty."

Jack frowned.

"Well, yes. Precisely. Yes it is, actually. Women are ruled by their biology and they're brilliant at passing all the shit onto us."

"And Amy doesn't want kids?"

"As if. In that respect she's a man. Did you want kids? Seriously. Was that why you got married?"

"No. But I was a willing convert. Once Michael was born, I kind of got into the groove. Sure, I miss Michael. I invested a lot of myself and look where that got me."

"Well, yeah. Precisely. We've been fools, Hugh. It's a total rip off."

"Hold on there. I don't think it's quite as bad as that. I'm not cynical, Jack. No other species is cynical about passing on genes."

"Sure, but look what the males do. They fuck off. In fact, their women don't want them around. We don't live naturally, Hugh. We live as we're *supposed* to live not as we actually are. Morality is the unnatural law."

"So you're going off to live like a gorilla. Well, good luck."

Jack shrugged.

"No. I don't know. To be honest, I haven't worked that out. Something in me just wants to be solitary. I'm tired, Hugh. I don't want to die yet, but I'm sick of it all. All the clutter, the ties, the rules. All the restrictions. We need to live more simply. I don't want to divorce Elise. I want to divorce the whole world. See? It's a much bigger thing."

"Well, I'm sorry, but to me that sounds like a midlife crisis. You want to wipe the slate clean and start again. You want to un-grow. Fact is we can't. You'll just find you're beating yourself up."

"No, no. That's not right. I don't want a second chance: get in a time machine and start again. No. I'm a guy, like any guy with a ton of shit on his back. Every day another piece of shit gets added. All I'm doing is raising myself back up and dumping the baggage. I don't want to be rude, but you're like everyone. They come running over tutting and shaking their heads and they start picking all the bags off the ground ready to load me back up. They use guilt, they use words like 'responsibility', 'duty' and 'obligation' and –"

"You got married. You signed up and followed through. Your goal was achieved twenty odd years ago."

"You too! Come on. Listen to yourself! We both made a mistake. I made a fucking big mistake. Big in my little life. Otherwise it means fuck all. Let it be small. Let it be as insignificant as it actually is. Shit, how I hate this puffed-up moral high ground guilt and indignation crap. Give me a break."

"Okay. Well, explain it all to your kids. Seriously, talk to them like you talk to me. Save them. Give them the foresight from your hindsight. Let your life be a warning to them. You know, Jack, I'm not really disagreeing with you. And you're right. I'm divorced. I screwed up. But Elise is not Marianne. Please, be kind and loving to Elise. You know, I'll be honest with you. She's a free spirit. She'd join you in your sailing away from it all if she could. But she can't break free. She's stuck back at base living up to her responsibility to your children. She's strong. Maybe she's patient."

Jack looked down, shook his head, and sighed.

"I know. Of course, I know that."

• • •

Jonah closed the front door as gently as he could.

"Jonah?" his mother called. She was in the front room. "Is that you, Jonah?"

"Yes. I'm just back."

There was no answer.

The boy hovered by the door, uncertain of what to do. It was late afternoon. She was normally calmer at this time of the day. Perhaps he should make the most of it and poke his head around the door. Instead he called back.

"Do you want any tea? I'm just making some."

He waited but there was no answer. She was ignoring him.

Jonah closed his eyes. He shrugged to himself and moved away from the front door. He'd make himself a mug of tea and go hide away in his room. If she got bad, he'd take himself off for a walk like usual. It was icy cold outside, mind. He longed for the spring. The longer evenings. The clocks would change next month and he'd go surfing.

• • •

Lie a person on their side and they become a landscape. Jack traced the soft hills of Amy's thighs, hips, the valley of waist rising to ribs and the peak of a shoulder. A cliff of clavicle, dipped throat, and shaded face. The light was perfect. Shadows and subdued highlights created an image between the realities of place and person. The work hovered before the eyes perfectly balanced like the faces of a Necker cube. The figurative was essentially abstract, even conceptual. Jack stepped back from the print on the white gallery wall. His eye scanned the edges for any imperfections or flaws in the production. It was fine. She was perfect. Jack folded his arms and smiled to himself. This was his favorite. The other photos were a little more figurative. He had allowed the balance to tip toward person; the image to the right was almost classical: breasts, bone, and velvet sheen of skin sliding softly into darkness. Erotic melting into plain sensuality. Light and dark. Amy.

"You okay in there, Mr. Rockshaw?"

Jack turned toward the voice. It brought him back to where he was. He saw the security guy at the gallery door, four-cell Maglite in hand.

"Thanks Ron. I'll be out any minute. I'll lock up."

The security officer raised his flashlight with a little wave and wandered on.

"Obfuscation," Jack muttered to himself. He looked around the gallery all set for tomorrow's opening. It felt like this would be the last exhibition; at least his last solo show. It was a secret farewell.

23

A week passed so slowly it was as if the late winter cold had frozen the hours. Hugh liked to walk along the coastal path, ever since that time with Elise. He'd walk as far as Pendour Cove and Zennor Head. From there you could see Patrick Heron's house, Eagle's Nest, a pale gray pile perched on a great outcrop of the landscape. For some reason it reminded him of a seashell: perhaps it was the color, the same forlorn emptiness. An artist's tall windows stared blankly out over the Atlantic swells, the black rocks, and the seagulls bending on the southwesterly gusts.

It was good to be in the big place and to see the broad back of the earth's edge. The wide view of the ocean.

Hugh liked Heron's work with its New York exuberance, pulsating shapes of color that were so removed from this dark coast – more California beach house than Eagle's Nest with its introverted gun grays, boggy browns, and tired greens. Hugh chuckled to himself. Where had all that color come from? The expansiveness and the sunshine. Why had Heron returned to Zennor when all others had fled? He had almost been the darling of the New York scene back in the sixties.

Hugh thought of Jack. Had the world changed so much? Would Jack have made more of an impression fifty years ago? Was his affair a symptom of his feelings of failure? From a distance, Hugh could see how it all just came down to being in the right place at the right time, or not.

Both he and Jack had somehow slipped off the edge of it all. The whole cynical Saatchi world of so-called Young British Artists – a corporate brand, not creative movement – was a dead pony, a shitty bed and it had no time for the likes of them. And he and Jack had been too absorbed in themselves and their own work to have looked up and seen what was going on and what it all meant. In their innocence and half-honesty, they had failed to see the changing landscape around them. Had Lawrence and Heron both gone to Australia, so far from here, in order to get a better perspective of what the hell was going on? Maybe he should do the same. Maybe he should have gone – Cornwall from London was certainly no Tahiti. Perhaps Jack had seen too much of his own life being so far away. And here they were now, each staring out into the Atlantic from their respective eyries. Both a little lost.

Hugh did know Jack better than he knew himself. He had the key. To be at the center of where or what you are is to be blind. I see every hill save the one I'm on and the reason we crave other people's attention is to find out a little more about who we are and maybe where we're heading.

• • •

Nigel Singleton turned his Yamaha moped down Soi Lam Promtep 3 to Rawai. Areeya's arms were clasped around him and he felt her head resting against his shoulder, knees touching the back of his legs, their skin sticky with the heat.

"I need to see Bruno about the boat. Won't take five minutes," he called back.

"It's good. I like Bruno. Then I can take you to my place. You must meet Tu. She's back from America last week to see her brother. I not seen her for a whole year."

"Sure. Okay. Sounds good."

They weaved their way through the sleepy village above the Rawai Beach resort. Nigel negotiated their way round speed bumps, dogs lying out in the road, children playing, and they traveled on down the other side of the small peninsula the other side of Nai Han. It was early evening and the raging humid heat of the day had lost its edge. Nigel felt that every pore of his body was sun soaked. The surf had been good, the sea as warm as a bath, and he could kill a Tiger beer right now. He could see the end of the winding road through the trees and they'd turn off at the bend for Paradise Beach bar. Bruno should be there waiting for them, maybe with some of his German Swiss friends. Markus was usually there.

He had arranged to have a look at a small fishing boat of Bruno's: nothing much, just a small outboard. He'd seen it from the bar a while back and Bruno had whined on about how he never went fishing 'no more' and what was the point of keeping 'zat zsing'. But it was a good boat and, in spite of its size, would get you out to the islands, even Ko Mai Thon but not Ko Racha Yai and that sort of gave him the measure of it. It was perfect for the coves and beaches, having a shallow draft. He'd had it made especially by a Canadian boat builder a few years ago who had come to retire but had gone again because of the heat and the boredom. What was that song? *Heaven is a place, a place where nothing, nothing ever happens.*

Sure enough, when they arrived, there was Bruno slouched on his usual bar stool, melting over his Bacardi and Coke. He was silhouetted against the sparkling silver blue of the sea beyond. The tide was low and there were locals right out in the bay collecting shellfish and checking nets. The cicadas buzzed with the sleepy heat. Areeya had already gotten off and was standing alongside. She was waiting for him.

"Nigel? What's the matter? Are you okay?"

He heard her voice and it sounded a long, long way away.

• • •

Amy didn't go to the exhibition's opening night. There would be all the faculty and other students and friends and critics, and she didn't want everyone ogling at her and Jack, labeling them as exactly what they probably were anyway, and then judging them, comparing their own moral worth and feeling smug or cool about it. Amy hated social gatherings.

Deep down she knew she would never be successful – in some accepted sense of the word – because she couldn't and wouldn't network. And she couldn't and wouldn't do what people like Jack seemed to do so naturally because she felt she shouldn't. Maybe she had gotten that from her father. He had little time for people, but that was because he didn't need to be sociable. He was a doctor. Having a profession removed any need to kiss ass. She envied that. She had inherited his attitude and his disdain but had none of the credentials, so she knew she was in big trouble and would certainly have – in some accepted sense – a tragic life. Which had come first: her dad's cold arrogance or his qualifications? She hoped very much that her father had been born contemptuous of people; otherwise, he truly was a pathetic man.

So Amy had arranged to meet Jack after the opening. They had agreed to meet at Barrio Chino's on Broome Street. Maybe they could walk back to Jack's apartment after. She was sitting at their table thinking alone to her margarita and had arrived half an hour late because she knew he wouldn't be there on time and he wasn't there now. Half past eleven. Moments like this reminded her how fucking annoying it was to be pretty and single. She wondered if her mother had got married just to end the hassle from jerks. She had been pretty too. And single. Was there a law somewhere that said you couldn't be both?

There was a guy groping toward the table.

"Hi. Sorry I'm late."

Amy looked up and there was Jack, who seemed a little breathless and he had that English lost look like they had never really got past post-war and what had happened back then in some other century or other. . .?

"You look confused. Did you lose something?" she asked.

Jack slid himself into the chair opposite that was up too close to the table but he couldn't push it back because there was someone yelling away at the next table banged up right close and that's always the way it is. Seeing his discomfort and that he glanced around with a frown warmed her. She smiled. She looked down at the table and gestured to pull it all toward her. Give the poor guy room to breathe.

"You need a big drink," she said. A waiter brushed up and she grabbed his attention. She just had to pin him with those frost blue eyes. So they were handy sometimes. Like now. "Hi. We need two anesthetics."

The waiter braked. He was one of those beefy overweight guys who maybe was into recreational bodybuilding but got the diet side all wrong. Like too much protein or whatever. There was too much noise and everyone so crushed in, the guy barely had any personal space. He raised his order pad close up to his chest.

"You need drinks?" he called down against the noise.

"Yes." Amy looked at Jack. She didn't want to lose the waiter while Jack dithered. "Two margaritas. Thanks."

"You got it. You ain't eating or nothing?"

"Sure. You choose. Whatever you think we should eat, we'll eat. How's that sound?"

The waiter looked at her for real this time. Then Jack.

Jack glanced at her and then the waiter.

"Um. Sure. Whatever."

"Yes. Whatever. It's all the same. Goes in one end, comes out the other, and, before it does, I guess we pay for it."

"Okay. I'll get you guys whatever."

Amy nodded approvingly and smiled over at Jack.

"Whatever sounds great. My favorite."

The waiter fought his way from the side of their table. Amy reached across and offered her hand.

"Whatever," said Jack, still mentally arriving.

"Yes. We live in a whatever culture. How did it go? Did anyone ask about me?"

Jack smiled and leaned toward her. He took her hand in his.

"Nope. They were too busy staring at you all spread out."

"Was I blushing?"

"No. But you should have been."

"Were you embarrassed for me?"

"No. I walked around with an oblivious erection."

"So it was a success."

Jack looked into her eyes and shrugged.

"See what the critics say."

"Did Jerry Salz turn up?"

"Nope. As if. Oh, there were some Twittering types. They're young enough to know better. God I hate the fuckers with their self-referencing ego-manic text speak shit. Someone needs to set up as a *critic* critic."

"No one listens to them anymore. Everything's online these days. No one pitches up to the gallery shows."

The waiter returned with their drinks.

"Two margaritas." He swooped their glasses down from a precariously held tray. "Whatever's on its way whenever."

Jack looked up and gave a wan smile. The waiter had already disappeared.

"Sure," said Jack, returning to their conversation. "Everything's fucked. Last time I was in New York there was a gallery on every street in Chelsea. Now it's all gone; swallowed up by Larry Gagosian and crowd and Paddle8, Artspace. The Russians just gobble up everything. It's a fucking meat market. I tell you, I'm out of this."

Amy frowned. Jack sounded serious.

"What do you mean?"

"That's my last show. No more. Maybe I'll just teach somewhere. I don't know."

"It's only New York. There are plenty of new colonies. Look at Berlin."

"That's not the point. It's the money. I can't do what these guys are doing now. I mean, the whole commercial thing. When I was a kid, the money side was an embarrassment. Everyone wanted to be poor. Bohemian. It was a badge of honor and integrity. Students now just don't get it. They've no idea what I'm talking about."

"I'm a student. I get it."

"You're not an art student. You're also not poor. How can art be any good when there's so much money around? How could there ever be a connection between price and value? It's just hyperinflation; hiking the price on a piece of shit doesn't change the shit.

"Yes it does. Of course it does."

"No one looks at the art. It's just the price tag. If Rembrandt was around today and gave his paintings away for free, no one would want them. Don't you see? The rich only understand dollar signs. The shit inside the frame is just a brand logo. I'm not exaggerating. That's really what's happening out there. It's nuts."

"Come on honey, you're just tired. It's been a hard day at the office. Anyway, look, we're meant to be celebrating."

Amy raised her glass for a toast.

Jack shook his head. He took his own cocktail and raised it with some reluctance.

"So, here's to your retirement!"

24

Elise was in the kitchen again when Hugh got back. It was as if someone had locked her in there. He didn't think she had seen him pass the window and he wondered if he should hide himself away in the studio. It was a house where people hid. It was like all houses.

He loitered near the back porch, a little indecisive, before deciding to head on up to the studio. He'd gotten a little wet from a short downpour on the lane coming back so needed to change anyway.

Maybe if he stomped past loud enough, she would hear he was back and she'd come out to find him. She would be keen to chat after his walk because he had been out with just his thoughts and that was as good to her as if he'd been out with friends comparing notes.

Poor Elise was a little lost, clinging to something that had fallen apart maybe several years ago. Did teenagers really understand or care how much damage they caused? Marriages were eggs. Perhaps because fathers were generally stood to one side of it all they were better at coping with the hatching process when it came. How could he help Elise reinvent herself? She would have to believe that he might hold the key and that he saw what she could not, as if he stood above the maze that trapped her.

So Hugh walked heavily away. He reached the side studio soon enough and opened the door. The air was cold and damp outside and his bedsit didn't feel much warmer. He felt he could do with a hot shower or a bath even just to infuse some heat into his stiff joints. His hands were numb and swollen. He took off his coat and went to sit on the end of his bed. Life felt painful. Literally, it hurt. With his coat over his knees, he lay back on the duvet and closed his eyes.

There was a tap at the door.

Hugh looked up.

"Yes. Door's open. I'm back," he called without rising. He spoke to the ceiling before turning his head at the opening of the door.

"I heard you come back."

"Come in. Sorry. Let me get up," Hugh replied, pushing himself onto one elbow. The coat fell off his knees onto the floor.

"You're tired. I'll come back later. Just came to ask if you wanted to eat with us this evening." Elise hovered at the entrance, reluctant to step in. Hugh sat up and rubbed at an eye.

"No come in. I'm fine. Are you okay?"

"We can talk later." Elise had started to turn away.

"No wait. I'll come now. It's cold in here; I forgot to leave the heater on. I'll come and join you in a second. I need a drink."

Elise glanced back and smiled. She nodded and closed the door.

Hugh listened to her muffled steps as she walked back to the house. He'd need to get some dry trousers on.

So she was desperate to talk. Perhaps there was news from New York.

He really had landed himself in it. He stood up and laughed gently at the irony of it all: his coming down to get away from the stress of family breakup only to find it waiting for him here. But this wasn't the cause of his problem with the Pieta. Far from it. In fact, in the past, all this would have fed him, fueled his creative energy. And he had really tried to make that happen this time, but it was all hopeless.

Hugh looked round for his corduroys. They were on the back of a chair beyond the bed. He went around to get them.

No, the problem with the Pieta was something quite separate. Of that, he was sure. But he was not at all certain about what he should say to Elise.

• • •

Jonah sat on the floor of his bedroom, leaning his back against the side of his bed. It was too cold to go surfing. Simon and the others were in town and he'd been asked along after school but he wasn't really in the mood. He had retreated to his room but he didn't feel like he was trapped. Not like other times. The gig at the Acorn had gone well enough the other day. Ian Weekes had even asked him about it.

Maybe his visits to the Rockshaw's barn had raised their estimation of him. People were strange. They reacted the opposite to what you were about. Like, if you wanted their friendship, they'd turn their backs. Walk away and do your own thing, then they were all over you. Jonah had already learned that he shouldn't live his life through other people. You continued on in spite of them. Bit like school. Bit like everything, really. So he sat there with his sketchbook, content enough, soft pencil poised over the page.

He had already been playing around with the Pieta. There were several sketches and doodles. It was the architecture of the icon that fascinated him: Mary sitting with this corpse draped over her knees like some monstrous, overgrown baby. This was the male vision. Semi erotic. Michelangelo's lean muscled Christ and young Mary all serene and thankful. Wasn't this more a confession of sexual repression? Michelangelo had been a hot-blooded twenty-five year old Italian male when he created the *Pieta* after all. Why was Mary so voluminously garmented, Christ so lovingly exposed? Why across her knees?

Jonah glanced down to the illustration in one of his art books from school. Fuck the religious iconography; Jonah was looking deeper into the revealed nature of the artist working within the conventions but exposing himself nevertheless.

Jonah looked away, in order to imagine what would be more realistic. Who would have dumped Christ onto her lap like that? She would be horrified, surely? War photos of mothers with dead sons were a million miles away from this. Of course, the great artist had wanted to emphasize the redemption and atonement and that this was a self-sacrifice and a positive thing. Jonah could see that there was absolutely no humanity in it at all. In many ways, the *Pieta*, the whole idea of the Pieta was monstrous. This was religion. It wasn't interested in humanity or love at all. Christianity had attempted to turn a tyrant into something loving like shoving a baby into Hitler's arms would make up for all the genocide and the hate. Given that God was just mankind's alter ego, all the nastiness and the cruelty were never far away, always just below the surface. And all that male obsession with female purity taken, with the Virgin Mary, to the ultimately absurd degree . . .

Jonah smiled as he realized what Mr. Borne had gotten himself into. There was no way he'd uncover what he was looking for in that rock. Then the smile faded. Should he say something? Was he allowed to say he felt sorry?

• • •

"So, did you have a nice walk?"

Hugh closed the porch door and wandered into the kitchen. It was dark outside and there was steam on the window. There was something cozy and reassuring about the busy bright whiteness, the pans on the stove, the closing of the fridge door.

"Hi. Yes, I did. I went as far as Zennor Head and had a good look at Heron's house up there. It always looks so abandoned. Sad in a way."

"Oh, it gets used quite a lot," said Elise, wiping her hands on a tea towel.

"You been?"

"Just once. All rather exclusive. Jack's been to a few weekend do's. Wine?"

"I'll get it. Sure."

Hugh walked across to the wine rack and removed a bottle he'd bought the other week.

"Here," said Elise, passing him a corkscrew. She seemed preoccupied. She was hiding behind preparing dinner. That's what domestic life was all about: distracting ourselves from the darkness outside. Wasn't that a good thing? Who'd want to be wandering the moors out there in the night with Grendel?

"Did you see anyone?" she asked, taking two glasses from the overhead cupboard and handing them to him.

"Not a soul. No one around until you got to America. But I didn't go that far."

Elise raised her eyebrows.

"Some do, or at least they used to. Before all the fish got eaten up. Now we're all marooned here."

Hugh nodded.

"We should light fires on the beaches and put notes in bottles. Not that I particularly want to be rescued."

Elise came over and pulled out a chair. Hugh was already sitting at the table wrestling with the corkscrew.

"Let me. Your hands are buggered. You'll drop the bottle."

Elise was right. He could hardly bend his fingers. He handed the bottle to her.

"Not that I particularly want to be rescued either," she said. "I read *Robinson Crusoe* the other week. I cried when he left the island." Elise spoke as she held the bottle and corkscrew like she was feeding a baby.

"Oh I agree. He was a king. And the novel just falls apart on his return to civilization. I never understood the ending."

"No," said Elise. She looked at him with curiosity and eased the cork out with a slight pop. Hugh pushed the glasses along the table toward her. She frowned as she poured. "We all get marooned one way or another. I think we got left in the wrong place. I mean, with all the others. The crowd."

Hugh smiled and nodded. He took his glass.

"Cheers. Yes, we did."

"Did Jack get marooned do you think?"

Hugh lowered his glass.

"He's passing by Ogygia that's all."

"Ridiculous book. Written by a man. How could an odyssey end with a return home?"

"Sure. I don't think it ends so much as stops. The myth of the epithalamion. It's odd when you think about it. It's as if we've been trying to cover up Genesis ever since. Marriage has been disastrous from year one."

Hugh looked up and saw that Elise was staring at him rather intently.

"What?" he asked.

She looked away.

"Nothing really. Well, what will you do after this? I've never asked you. It seems strange that the winter is passing and life is coming back to a different landscape."

"Has Jack been in touch?"

Elise nodded.

"Yes. A couple of weeks' time. That's going to be fun, isn't it?"

"And the kids don't know."

"No."

Hugh leaned forward a little and looked into his glass.

"Then maybe it will blow over. It's good you're both talking." He looked up. "Will you give him a chance? I mean, if he realizes what a dick he's been?"

"*Me* give him a chance? Oh, I thought it was meant to be the other way around?"

"Well, you know what I mean."

"I think you defend him, actually. Men together in this battle of the sexes."

"No. Not at all. Actually, I was thinking there's no reason why you can't both escape. He's not running from you so much as from all *this*." Hugh looked round at where they were.

"Oh, you mean children and responsibility."

"It's not like that. It is about offspring, though. In a way. I mean, when the fruit ripens, the flower dies. If there is such a thing as a midlife crisis, it's about that. It's a rebellion against the tyranny of our biology."

"That's bloody nonsense, Hugh. We're not cherries."

"No. We're not. So we should stop behaving as though we were."

"We're mammals. I nurture the young and Jack goes and gets the meat."

"And that process takes a quarter of our lives away. Maybe a third. The best years of our lives sold into slavery. And it's not the kids' fault. It's a cultural thing. It's the way we have become. We're more like drones or worker ants. Everyone is slaving away for the good of what?"

"So maybe we should go and sail round the world."

"Sure. Why not? You know, you have a lot of capital tied up here. And there's the shop."

"Just sell it all up. So that's what I say to Jack when he returns."
Elise laughed. "Well, that would certainly call his bluff and test your theory too. I'd love to see his face when I'm standing there with Simon and Caja, clutching our bags and blankets all ready. So, Jack, where we going?"

"You don't have to go with him, Elise. Just ask him for a lift to the airport."

25

"What are you going to do?"

"I don't know. Smash it all to pieces."

"And start again."

Jack looked round sharply. The alcohol had made the streetlights dance. He shook his head and raised his finger at her.

"No. Now there's the secret. I worked it out. The thing is, the thing is to keep it all flat. Just all level and don't build anything over again. Keep it flat, Amy. D'you hear what I'm saying?"

"Keep it flat, Jack."

"That's right, flat and empty."

"Empty. So you're going to live in a hedge or something. Be a hobo. Push a Wal-Mart shopping cart round New Jersey with your stuff in it."

"No cart. No streets."

"Back to nature."

Jack nodded too enthusiastically.

"Yes. Exactly."

"Go to Alaska and live with the wolves."

"No wolves."

"They'd eat you up. We're poodles, Jack. Step beyond the suburbs and we're dead meat. You going to be the next Chris McCandless?"

"Who?"

"You know, the guy who hitchhiked into the scary wild place and ended up dead. Nature's a murderer."

"Are you serious?"

"What? About what?"

"You really see nature as a killer? So what's this? What's all *this* shit?" Jack stepped away from Amy, toward the edge of the sidewalk. He waved his drunken arms."

"Okay Jack. Let's get home. I'm cold. You're drunk. I don't know what's upsetting you."

Jack wheeled back. He put his arm round her and spoke with puffed clouds of alcohol.

"You're right. Everything's out to kill us."

"Sure Jack. It's called life. Life's a real killer."

Jack nodded heavily.

"Okay, I got it this time. The secret is to make sure that in the three score years and ten it takes us to die, we die sublimely. Dying should be fun, right?"

"Sure. With you it's fun. That's why we're together. Like right now . . ."

Jack removed his arm and stopped. Amy stopped too after a couple more paces.

"Jack?" She turned and looked back. "You okay?"

She looked down and removed her glove. Then she reached into her coat pocket and returned to him.

"Here. You need this. It's the last tissue I got."

• • •

It was the last weekend in February. Hugh had just come back from a walk down to the end of the lane. It was a bright blustery morning and there was a tentative hint of spring in the still wintry air. The light was changing and, to the expert eye of an artist, perhaps, the gray of the sea now had a hint of cerulean: one part to a hundred.

Hugh walked along the side of the house from the front drive and then along the path to the studio. Jonah was at the door waiting for him. The boy smiled shyly on seeing him approach.

"Morning Mr. Borne. I thought you might be out. I came early."

Hugh smiled back and shook his head.

"I went for a walk. I've been thinking all week about today." He went straight to the door and reached for the handle. He glanced at Jonah who had moved from leaning against the wall and was now coming to join him. Hugh lifted the latch and continued to talk as they entered. "Yes, I've made some big decisions. You know things have been heading this way."

Jonah followed Hugh in and closed the door. They both walked on up to the stone and the emerging figures. They looked in silence for some time almost as if they were connecting to each other.

"What is it?" asked Jonah.

Hugh sighed.

"Listen, I'm not defeated by this. I'm making a stand, that's all."

"A stand? What do you mean?"

Hugh took his eyes off the sculpture and looked at Jonah.

"At my age you sometimes forget yourself. You forget where you came from at the beginning of where you now stand. Once I was like you. Everything was driven by expectation. We start life as explorers. Eventually, we discover all that we set out to find and the magic fades and we become defined by what we came to conquer. I'm not a Christian. I'm not a catholic. This means nothing to me. Of course it doesn't, and I should have realized. When I was younger I would have been dumbfounded by this."

Hugh wandered up to the rock and reached out to touch the cold granite.

"It's just a monster. It was never meant to be."

"They're all monsters," said Jonah coming up alongside.

Hugh frowned then raised his eyebrows.

"Really?"

"Yes. The image is based on a lie. Religious art is sort of twisted. It's always corrupted. It doesn't portray truth ever, only dogma. It enslaves the spirit of the artist. Love between people just isn't like this. Did you see that sculpture of Christ as a homeless guy on a bench? You know the one the church turned down because it wasn't appropriate?"

"The Tim Schmalz bronze? Sure. I heard about that. And you're right. Christians don't love Jesus because he was a poor nobody but because he was the son of a god. Religion is all about power."

There was a silence.

"What are you going to do?"

"Nothing."

"Nothing?"

"I stop. It's finished. Too much pain and too much delusion. I'm not adding to it anymore."

Jonah didn't reply. He was too busy soaking up the sculptor's words and the situation. Hugh went over to the table of tools and looked down.

"So you'll be leaving. What will happen to the stone? What's going to happen?"

"I go away poorer than I came," said Hugh, lifting a grinder and wrapping the electric cable round the handle. "I'll write to the convent and tell them. They'll have to get someone else to do their work. I'll get back some feeling of integrity at least. It's worth it. But I can't do this anymore. Maybe I'll take some time out. Get back to painting again. Go to France this summer."

Jonah hovered nervously. He cleared his throat.

"You said you'd let me maybe do something. Remember? I mean, I was really thinking about this. All week. I made a load of sketches and stuff. I can show you."

Hugh was listening. He lowered the grinder in his hands and rested it on the table.

"Yes. I did, didn't I?" He looked at Jonah. He shook his head. "I don't want to be negative, but you'd bounce off that rock. Seriously. It's like cast iron. You've never touched a chisel. Forget it. Anyway, the project's finished. I'm packing up and going . . . Where am I going? Well, I'm just going."

"Then maybe I can practice. You know, just have a go."

"You haven't got any tools. You need all *this* stuff."

"You're not going right now. When are you leaving? You just decided now. Maybe you'll change your mind."

Hugh smiled at Jonah's persistence. His enthusiasm.

"See? You're an explorer. Hmm."

"What?"

"Well, no harm in giving you a chisel and, here, this mallet will do. Let you have a play around. Sure." Hugh shrugged and lifted the tools off the table. He turned them in his hands.

Jonah stepped closer. He wanted to see.

"Can you show me some things? Just some basics."

Hugh lowered the tools back onto the table.

"Okay, look, maybe I need to think about this more. To be honest, Jonah, I'm all over the place. I can't do this piece but I don't want to just give in like this. I gave so much of myself to this project. It's a disaster, really, and I should be more fucked up about it than I am. It's weird. You know, I've noticed that I can make a piece and it can take months to get right and then, once it's done, I don't give a shit about it. I'm like a chef. I'll spend days getting a dish to perfection just to have it eaten in minutes. Do I cry about that? Of course not."

"So this is the same?" asked Jonah.

"No. That's the problem. It's not the same. It's not finished. I'm sort of stuck in Limbo. You only trash what you make when it's done. So, I don't know what to do. I'm stuck."

Jonah hung his head slightly.

"I see. Well, shall I make some coffee at least?"

Hugh smiled and touched Jonah on the shoulder.

"Cheer up. You look well pissed off. Jonah, don't worry, I'll come up with something. Okay? It's not easy. I'm sorry."

Jonah frowned and moved away.

"I'm fine. It's nothing really. Don't ask you don't get. That's what my dad used to say."

Hugh folded his arms and nodded solemnly.

"That's true. Let's have coffee. Let's make time. Time, time, time. Slow this down."

Jonah began to turn.

"Jonah?"

"What?"

"Do you miss your father? I wish you would tell me about him. Would you do that for me?"

Jonah seemed to freeze.

"Why?"

"Why not? Because I'm interested. I'm a dad too, you know. I want to find some things out. Go make the coffee. It's time we talked."

Jonah didn't answer but moved to the door, opened it and left.

Hugh looked at the Pieta. He felt it stood there like a condemned animal staring back innocent of its fate and a little self-conscious. Was there any way he could save this? He started to walk round the stone. He looked with impartial, disinterested eyes and tried to turn the so familiar scars of his labor into foreign, unknown marks that meant nothing to him, but it was difficult. This was work in progress. He hated to have to leave it like this, but what could he do? If he completed it, he would have contributed to the world nothing more than a hideous thing that would not fade with time; no scrap thieves would be able to haul it from its pedestal to melt it down. The granite would continue to defy the elements for hundreds of years beyond his own passing like some god-awful tombstone. No, it could not go on, that was for sure.

So what next? Should he go to London and pack up? He needed to get away. St. Ives had really brought him nothing but sore hands.

He sighed and went to sit on a deck chair over by the far wall. He lowered himself heavily, his knees a little stiff from the walk earlier. He looked across the studio at the wreckage of a winter. Perhaps it might look good as an unfinished piece emerging from the rock like a Rodin. But no. It was a mess of deformed stone ready for a scrapyard or a builder's tip.

The door opened and distracted Hugh from his thoughts.

"I'm back here," he called. His breath condensed on the cold damp air and his voice echoed slightly. He heard the door close and then saw Jonah coming over round the Pieta with their coffees steaming.

"So, Jonah. Your father. Tell me about him. Do you think about him?"

Jonah shrugged. He stepped up and handed Hugh his coffee. The artist shifted.

"Sorry, there seems to be only one chair."

"It's all right. I'll sit on the floor. I can lean against the wall just here."

Jonah carefully put his mug down on the wooden floor and then lowered himself.

"Thanks. This is just what I needed," said Hugh.

"I don't know what you want me to say? I don't usually talk about him." Jonah sighed. "Do I have to?"

Hugh looked down and smiled.

"I'd like you to. You see, I have a son about your age. I divorced and he went with his mother. It's what happens these days."

"Don't you see him?"

Hugh shifted a little and the chair creaked.

"It's early days but you know what, I don't think I'll be seeing him for a long time at the best. They went back to Paris. My ex-wife's family lives there. So you see . . ."

"That's too bad. I'm sorry."

"It's okay. It's just odd. You know, it's not what you planned to happen and then it happens just like that."

There was an uncomfortable moment of silence before Jonah spoke.

"It was, um, because of my mum, really. He'd had enough. Well, he was always sort of doing his own thing. He was a keen surfer."

"Where did he go?"

"I don't know. He just left us. Literally walked out and never came back. That's what really hurt me. You know, being dumped. Wasn't my fault, was it."

"No. I'm sorry to hear that. He must miss you."

"Yeah, right."

"No, really. Remember, I'm a father with a son your age. I can tell you for sure, he will be feeling like shit right now. He'll wake every morning and think of you before getting on with his day. That's how it is."

"I don't think so."

"Why?"

"Why doesn't he contact me? He doesn't write or anything. It's like I died."

HALF-MOON ISLAND, CUCKOO TOWN, FROM 'THE DARK MONARCH', 1962
SVEN BERLIN

MARCH

26

"You're leaving next week?"

"Elise, I never planned to stay beyond March."

"But the Pieta's not ready. I hoped you'd see Jack."

"I am seeing Jack. We're meeting up in London."

Elise looked pained. She shook her head.

"I don't understand why you're rushing off like this. It doesn't make any sense."

"It's been six months, Elise."

"But the Pieta. What about Jonah?"

Hugh watched Elise lower herself onto the chair at the kitchen table. He knew how much she had depended on him. His being there had filled a gap and had held her world together somehow. He could see how she was now turning things over in her mind to adjust to or catch up with reality.

"I'm sorry."

"Hugh, it's not about Jack. I mean, why are you rushing off like this?"

"I've told you. I'm not rushing off. Look, the Pieta hasn't worked out. I screwed it up, didn't I?"

"Is that my fault? Is it because of me and Jack?"

Hugh frowned. It hadn't occurred to him that the crisis in the Rockshaw family might have been the cause of his problem with the Pieta. He shook his head and went to join Elise at the table.

"No. Of course not. Actually, Jonah and I talked it through at the weekend. The boy's pretty perceptive about things."

"He's very sensitive. He'll be distraught you're leaving."

"Well, I don't know. He saw the problem with religious art. The dogma. I should never have taken this on. It was all about paying solicitors. Nothing good was ever going to come out of that. I've freed myself. It's liberating to turn away from something that's not right. It was a great big lie."

"It's all a great big lie. The rest of us deal with it. Why can't you?"

"What's *that* supposed to mean? Look, Elise, I can't help you. It's between you and Jack. I'm not going to get caught up in what's happened."

Elise looked at him carefully.

"I helped you. I supported you didn't I?"

Hugh couldn't meet her eyes. He looked down at his hands.

"I'm seeing Jack in London. I want to talk to him away from here. It's sort of why I'm going back next week. And listen, I'm doing it for you. For you both. Don't you want to save your marriage? Of course, I didn't really think of that. I assumed you would. You should. Jack has been ridiculous. He's got a massive climb down to face and I want to help him. Elise, you're the strong one. He's the one who needs help."

"And you believe all that, do you?" Elise asked after a pause.

"Whatd'ya mean? Of course I believe that. Jack's a mess. If he came straight back here it would be a disaster."

"You were on his side. Before. I mean, you didn't seem that bothered about saving our marriage."

"That's not true. Elise, I said I didn't see why you had to be collateral damage. Jack's looking for freedom from this place not from you. If you can both find a new way of living that's more honest, more authentic, then why split?"

"Is that what you're going to say to him?"

"Given the chance, yes. Sort of. Look, I spoke to Jonah about his father. He opened up a bit. You know what he said?"

"What?"

"When parents split up, the pain isn't over losing a parent it's seeing your parents lose each other. He talked about the Pieta. He wanted to change the figures: not Mary and Jesus but Mary and Joseph. There's too much attention on kids and parents in divorce. Maybe there should be more thought given to the loss of the love that started it all. I think you can save your marriage. Really. I've known you and Jack for so long. Right back to Falmouth. Marianne and I should never have got married. You and Jack should have done. It was always the right thing and still is. So it's got to be saved.

"If I can help, I will. I have to go back next week. Can you change your life? Put the two of you first rather than the kids?

"You know what? I reckon if you put your relationship with Jack back to where it was before you had children, Simon and Caja would be transformed. They'd think you were amazing. How cool and how rare to have parents who loved each other more than them and who were first class citizens again not slaves to their progeny? Grownups first. Kids second. It's a heresy, I know, but that's what I've learnt. That's what I've seen."

• • •

Amy stretched her naked length across the bed with a gesture so self-assured it was defiant, like a diver thrown out over the water. It wasn't a pose. It wasn't particularly self-conscious. It was genuine and in a way innocent or primitive, as though there was no one looking and it made Jack feel he wasn't there at all and that he didn't exist. There was a vestige of a child in her limbs as if the bones were still pliably soft and light, like a bird's; he watched the way her toes reached out and sent a little tremulous wave up her legs to open the backs of her knees, a firming of buttocks, skipping fingers up each notch of her spine and the downward tilt of her head, her arms up-stretched and the rigid spasm at her fingertips. He was overwhelmed by a sensation of déjà vu and the stretching of his soul.

• • •

Jonah couldn't face the day in school. When he had reached the turn off, he carried on right past and headed for Carbis Bay. He wanted to spend the morning on the vast acreage of sands below Lelant that sprawled out to the Hayle estuary and slipped shallow under the rippled carpet of the sea.

It was a place that haunted him. That the great ocean curved by the bay should be halted by an inch of elevated sand fascinated him. That the power to smash a great ship could be held in check by such a delicate balance of forces was a miracle worthier of his contemplation.

But there was something else that had Jonah now hiving off toward the coastal path that beetled along the rocky cliffs between the railway line and the sea. It was the sensation of a time coming to an end. The edge of things. Spring had appeared like a border checkpoint beyond which winter could not pass and was not welcome. But Jonah would travel on through the seamless divide because he was a ghost. Mr. Borne would be stuck in the memory of the barn and the Pieta and a brief period in a short life that had yet to lengthen and broaden.

It is only the old who regret the passing of the days. There is some brief light at the center of one's life to which the young hasten. But that high summer, with the long days hanging indolently into the late evenings, once reached passes barely noticed for our complacency and ever-distracting toil. Jonah knew all this. He would hold the sensuality of each and every hour if he could. There were such precious departures, such perpetual mournings.

• • •

Elise was late opening the shop.

She had left Hugh sitting at the kitchen table a little surprised to see her get up rather suddenly and exclaim how she had forgotten the time: she'd be late and it would be a pain trying to find a parking space.

So she had driven off annoyed with herself and at Hugh.

It all felt like a conspiracy. Why had Hugh not consulted her over his meeting Jack in London? That was a bit arrogant, wasn't it? Was he acting on her behalf or Jack's? It wasn't as though she had asked him to speak for her and, besides, he didn't know what she wanted. She didn't know herself what she wanted. Bloody men. She had a mind to tell them all to fuck off.

She knelt down to pick up the bills and junk mail from the mat behind the door and she turned away from the front of the shop but not before something had caught her eye. A movement. A person.

She felt compelled to open the glazed door and step out onto the cobbled street outside. There was no one else around. She glanced up the lane and then back down to the woman she had seen and whose back was now some distance down the way. The lady was stooped and walking furtively toward the Digey.

"Mrs. Singleton! Mrs. Singleton?" she called. The figure hesitated.

Encouraged, Elise hurried after her, leaving the gallery door ajar. She walked briskly on and Mrs. Singleton turned to face her.

"Hello. You're Jonah's mother. I've seen you pass before. I wanted to say how much we've enjoyed having Jonah over to Zennor."

Mrs. Singleton frowned and there was an awkward pause.

"Well, I hope it's been a help. He has such a talent, you –"

"You're Elise Rockshaw. I know."

"Yes."

"Mr. Rockshaw is a fine artist. He's famous, isn't he?"

Elise stepped back and looked down.

"He's a photographer. Hugh Borne has really taken to Jonah."

"Has he?"

"Oh yes . . . Look, would you like a coffee? I've got coffee back at the gallery."

"Oh no. I'm busy. Always I'm busy." Mrs. Singleton began to turn away.

It filled Elise with such pain and she wanted to cry out with anger. But she didn't. She stood by helplessly silent and let Jonah's mother go. Mrs. Singleton reminded her of a fox she had once disturbed on the coastal path below the house. It had leapt out of the gorse onto the track just in front of her and had given her a backwards glance that was the merest flick of an eye but it had buried a dart of wild sadness deep into her heart.

27

The world is young for the young and old for the old.

• • •

Gone to Gutai exhibition. See you there at 11.30?

Jack lowered Amy's note and glanced over to the travel clock on the bedside cabinet. What time was it? She had mentioned going to the Guggenheim. He had forgotten and now had woken up late and she had gone. He had an hour to get there, rush uptown like a maniac, and go chasing after her.

The final days of his time here and with Amy were turning into a work of performance art. He should video it all and shove it onto a big screen at MoMA. Chop it up a bit, maybe. Some in black and white, parts played backwards, and all jerky and odd angles here and there. What should he call it? 'Sublimity'?

Pursuit was the unrequited love between traveling and arriving. Arrival was the horizon, the place you should never reach beyond the edge, and the opposite of the focal point.

He had learned to despise art. It was only ever about demanding your attention. The egotist and the narcissist wanted only to draw you into the center of themselves whilst pretending it was just about the world beyond, the world from which they had pulled you. But all he wanted to do was look more carefully at the wall, the view beyond the billboard, because he knew the game they were playing and it bored him. If art was about pulling you into itself then, in that respect, it did imitate life and gravity was everywhere sucking at you to stay and be owned.

He loved Amy because she was unattainable and beyond the possible; always beyond the fringe of his vision, of his life, and she would be a constant reminder to him that to arrive was to die.

And travel? What was that? Expectation? Hope? If there was no such thing as carnal desire, no one would board trains or climb into cars. There would be no planes, no traffic jams, no legs for walking; people would become rooted like plants.

All human activity was ultimately driven by a lust to conceive the *petite mort.*

Jack looked away from himself. He should get a move on and was running out of time. It was no good standing there naked in front of the mirror contemplating his navel. Gutai. Splendid play.

By the time he arrived at the Guggenheim, it was twelve forty. He spotted Amy almost immediately. She was standing on the floor of the rotunda looking up, her gold hair hanging down. Artifice and the natural were held in a combined moment of suspense. Jack glanced at the web of Motonaga Saganasa's installation draped and crisscrossing the white glare of the atrium above their heads. Amy hadn't spotted him.

"Hello. You know *that's* a joke," he said as he approached.

Amy turned and looked at him with calm surprise.

"You came," she said.

"You left."

"I didn't want to wake you."

He didn't reply and they both looked up again, this time as one.

After a while, Jack spoke.

"The whole point was that it should be outside. You know, taking art out of the art space into reality. Good to see they got it back in the vault. Are you done?"

Amy removed her eyes from the polyethylene tubes hanging there.

"Do you think they look like brush strokes?" she asked.

"No."

"Me neither."

"They look like plastic pipes with puddles of colored water. But to people it doesn't matter. No one cares what they're looking at. It's just stuff in a Pinterest world. Maybe there was an idea once but it's gone. Can we go? I hate it here."

Amy frowned slightly, then nodded.

"Sure. Okay. I'm done."

"Good."

They left through the Guggenheim shop. Jack hovered as the thought he should pick something up for the kids flapped through from one side of his mind to the other. Amy had already gone. She was standing beyond the glass, watching the tourists wash in and out of the museum. Jack refocused and made for the exit. Amy turned and smiled to him.

"Is 'cute' the same as 'cutesy'?" she asked as he came up.

"That's random." Jack took her hand in his and looked down at her fingers. She laughed.

"You looking for an answer?" She removed her hand gently. "There's something kitsch about Japanese taste. All that Harajuku kawaii stuff."

"You think Gutai is kitsch?"

"Sort of. Fancy lunch somewhere? You know, it's almost nice enough for a picnic in the park. Don't you think?"

"It's not snowing, if that's what you mean. I need a drink. Let's go to that Italian place on East Fifty-Eighth."

"Okay."

Amy led the way slightly ahead, as she always did. It annoyed him because he wanted to talk and she didn't seem that interested. He stepped out to catch up alongside her.

"God, you walk so fast. Look, I'm sorry if I dismissed the exhibition. Was I too disrespectful? Let's talk about it if you want. You wanted to go, so why was that? I didn't know you were into Japanese art."

Amy glanced at him and slowed just a little.

"I'm not really." She left it at that and they walked on.

"There's nothing cute about Gutai. There's a sort of animist feeling about it. You know, like *kami* is embedded in the artifact. Yoshihara talks about how artists murder materiality. I don't think kawaii culture has any connection. But I haven't thought about that really. You're not listening, are you?"

Amy nodded. She put her arm in his and leaned toward him.

"I am. I'm thinking you seem tense. Why's that?"

"Am I tense?"

"Yes, you are."

Jack thought about how he was feeling. He tried to observe himself. She was right. Of course he was tense. Rather magically, he knew this was the last time he would see her. He had three days left in New York and she wouldn't be there at the very end. This was the end she had devised for him, the outermost edge of what they had been. He knew that, and there was a secret, unspoken deal between them that they wouldn't mention anything about his leaving. It was almost one of her games. But he was allowed to feel annoyed wasn't he? There was the line between them she had drawn so defiantly that time. How long ago that now seemed.

"Amy?"

She didn't slow this time but she looked at him with eyes that said: no last cigarette. No blindfold.

"Oh Jack, I want you to tell me all about Yoshihara and the bomb and keeping it all level and flat. Empty. Okay?"

She gave his arm a barely perceptible squeeze and he realized then that she had lined herself up against the same wall. It was kind of her.

They sat by the window. A waiter gave them menus and Jack ordered the wine straight away. He leaned toward Amy across the table as she was deciding on what to have.

"Do we have to talk about art? I'd rather talk about you."

Amy glanced over the top of the menu in her hands then carried on reading.

"I'd rather talk about art. Anyway," she said, lowering her menu, "they're connected aren't they? I mean, people and art."

Jack shrugged and leaned back again.

"I don't know, maybe. You know, the fact is I don't care anymore."

"Okay, so do you think, in some unconscious way, the Gutai artists were responding to the war? I mean, wow, they got pretty obliterated, right?"

She spoke as if the last century was a long, long time ago. She must have been seven at the turn of the millennium. She had missed the whole of the Cold War. He felt suddenly so old. Had he been so blind to the great void of time between them?

"They got *obliterated*? Did you ever hear of CND?"

Amy looked vacantly at him and shook her head.

"Fuck."

"Oh yeah, yeah, no I did. Sure, CND. And that peace sign. I missed out, right?"

Jack smiled and nodded.

"You know what? Yes, I think you did. Young people were different then. Young people were sort of young, you know, new. Now they're old. They're like me, bored and cynical. The world has become middle aged. I mean, what turns you on? What are you fighting for?"

Amy looked a little vacant but Jack continued.

"Technology has turned everyone into a voyeur. There are layers and layers of microprocessors between us and what's going on. It's a slow, rather distant death."

Amy frowned.

"Okay. So I'll hitchhike to Alaska." She looked down. "I wasn't part of that world. It must have been awesome. Sure, I couldn't sell my world to you so easily. It's a bit pathetic. Maybe I need a midlife crisis."

The waiter returned with a bottle of Montepulciano d'Abruzzo. Jack smiled.

"I'm sorry. I must sound like a teacher. Okay, so you wanted to talk about art."

The waiter was ready to let Jack taste and he hovered over them.

"It's fine, just pour. Please. Thanks," said Jack. He leaned back and the waiter filled their glasses.

"Ready to order?"

Jack and Amy looked at each other.

"Um . . . "

Amy shook her head.

"Okay. I'll be back when you're ready." With that, the waiter left them.

"Art."

Amy sighed.

"Maybe we shouldn't. It just seems to make you angry. Unhappy."

"Not really. It bores me. Maybe that's what happens when it's your job. Like conductors hate the sound of music in their homes. And there you have it. When something is so familiar and workaday, the center of your existence, it becomes this dead weight. Midlife crisis is the dead weight of all the crap you've managed to accumulate around yourself in five decades. We're a species of hoarders. We hoard the years with stuff. Yoshihara was wrong, we don't murder materiality, materiality murders us. The great postwar Japanese miracle was defined by stuff. They should never have rebuilt the bombed cities. It was all a tragic losing of memory. Look at all those cities in Europe rebuilt exactly as they had been before the bombs as if nothing had happened. Dresden, Tokyo, Nagasaki were works of art sculpted by ordnance. Now look at them."

Amy smiled and raised her glass.

"To destructive creativity."

Jack raised his own glass.

"To creative destruction."

• • •

Amy's father, Doctor Rosenberg, was standing on the corner of Freiburgstrasse in front of the Inselspital. He was waiting for his mistress, Elodie, to bring the car round. She had wanted to take him to the airport and see him off. They would drop by the hotel and pick up his bags from the concierge. It was kind of her but a little awkward.

He raised his wrist and glanced at his watch. It had been an agreeable conference. Good to see Hans Breitel again after all these years. Elodie had been sweet and she had kept away from talking about her husband and offloading her life and how bored she was in Berne. How it was killing her. "Wasn't Switzerland one of the most desirable countries in the world to live?" he had said. And Berne, the old quarter at least, was delightful. She was so lucky to live in such a quaint and dignified town, to have such a loving husband, and three great kids.

No, this time she had kept off the topic of where life had taken her. It was as if their hours together were too precious to waste and that she wanted to wring them for all the escape they might afford. She had learnt that from him. Why spend the whole time in heaven ranting on about hell? Where was the escape in that? They had fucked with a greedy desperation that had bordered on madness.

28

Young people's image of our past is a forgotten memory of a place they've never seen. There is little recompense to be found in a world where, for some brief time, we shall be absent in their own later lives. And yet we were young and we are what our children will become. Should we tell them that nothing changes and that there's nothing new of what really matters?

• • •

Hugh lowered the last of his tools into the holdall and he had to admit to himself that just this final gesture brought home the sense of defeat and of having given up. He had been so close to this sort of moment in the past but, upon the point of walking away, he had always turned back and carried on. The lows had almost possessed a creative energy of their own: dark and brooding. But not anymore, it would seem. He was giving up on so much more than the Pieta. In the past, he would have been terrified to be doing this. But he felt a calm that eventually comes. Creative energy need not be so bipolar and Hugh felt he had emerged from the winter into the stable state that said you don't have to keeping proving you can do this.

Who was he trying to kid? He stepped back a little and kicked the bag.

"Shit. Shit. Shit!"

There was a cough from beyond the door. Hugh stopped immediately and looked round. Was Elise back for something? Then he saw Jonah. Hugh felt suddenly rueful and then a little resentful at having his privacy disturbed. This was a major moment in his life and he hardly wanted to be forced into exchanging pleasantries.

Jonah stood in the doorway, dimming the light into the studio. Hugh stepped round so that the stone wasn't blocking his line of sight.

"Hello Jonah. Aren't you meant to be in school?" Hugh then wondered if perhaps there was some big problem. Why was the boy here on a weekday?

Jonah remained at the door.

"I was wandering by."

Hugh began to walk round.

"You were wandering by? Like from St. Ives to Zennor is a minor detour. You okay?"

The boy nodded unconvincingly. He glanced at the Pieta and Hugh saw his eyes travel shyly to the holdall and the cleared table. He felt like a thief, or worse.

"Let's have a coffee. This time I'll make it. You can tell me what you're doing here."

Jonah turned and stepped down onto the path back to the house when Hugh reached the doorway.

"I couldn't face school again. I can't bear it sometimes. The teachers. The whole thing. All those petty rules. As if no one could learn anything without it all. You know what, Mr. Borne?"

They started walking round to the side studio.

"What?"

"I don't learn anything. I want to learn so much and all that happens there is I'm kept away from what I need to know. I can't explain."

Hugh sighed.

"What do you need to know?"

Jonah stopped and looked round.

"Everything. Life. The world as it is. I'm not dissing school or anything, but I feel it all here." Jonah put his fist against his chest.

"Are you okay Jonah?"

The hand was lowered. The boy looked at the ground.

"Yes."

"Okay. Look. You need school. You need education. A good deal of the world, of life is actually pretty conventional. All of that will be lost to you. Reject it later. Sure. Don't reject things in advance. Call me an old empiricist but there's something to be said for trying things out first. You know, it annoys me when people say they hate this or that without having given it a go to inform their opinion. It's just plain prejudice. It's not attractive, Jonah."

They had reached the door and Hugh went in first. He wiped his feet on the mat and switched on the light. Jonah hovered again.

"Come in. Here, and close the door, it's freezing."

"What's an empiricist?"

Hugh smiled and went over to the kettle. He lifted the lid to check there was enough water.

"Well, there you go. That's the sort of thing you learn in school. You'll not learn how to articulate your thoughts without language. No language, no thinking. The clouds and the waves won't teach you how to think. You might feel things in your heart, but the head. The mind, Jonah. The mind." Hugh looked at the boy and tapped his finger against his temple.

"Then I can read in the library. Don't you see? School stops me reading. It stops me thinking. I don't want to be a fucking bank clerk. So if you're an empiricist, tell me what you found out. Was school worth it?"

Hugh frowned. He stepped back and sat on the edge of the bed.

"Sure. That's a fair question. I've thought about all that. I was very much into the naïve, you know, primitivism. I loved Wordsworth as a boy. John Clare. And all the artists, of course. The thing is, a lot of those who criticized formal education had all received some form of education. I mean, you know that whole Pink Floyd Brick in the Wall thing is pretty suspect, isn't it? God, I don't know. It's complicated. The fact is Jonah, I wasn't brilliant enough. I needed the system. Maybe you don't. I wasn't willing to take the risk and I didn't want to be some kind of outcast. An outsider. Have you read any Larkin?"

Jonah shook his head.

"You should. Well, I'm like Larkin. Read his poem called *Toads.* Sad thing about Larkin was he was a genius but not a great man. An odd combination. There was something wonderfully trapped. Freedom terrifies us as much as death. Sven Berlin, on the other hand was no genius but he had a greatness in a way. Sure, he must be a real hero for you. He was one of the last of the heroes really. That whole post war generation going off and living with the gypsies. All that death and destruction had forced people to live a little more honestly, briefly at least – before the factories returned from making tanks to churning out cars and cookers and everyone got back in their boxes again."

The kettle had boiled and there was a silence. Jonah moved to the desk below the window and he sorted out the mugs and coffee.

"Think big. You will make your decisions whatever people say. Be good at something. That's all. Maybe that's the problem with school. It doesn't set out to make people good, you know, talented at something. Just mediocre across the board. Well, you can leave at the end of this year."

Jonah poured and remained thoughtfully silent. He lowered the kettle and added the milk. He picked up their mugs and handed one to Hugh.

"Thanks."

"Mr. Borne. I want to finish the Pieta. Will you give me the chance? You're going soon. Can you show me a few things? You said, that time, you would."

Hugh lowered his mug and looked up.

"I did, didn't I? There's not much time. You need tools. What are you going to do with it?"

"I just need a bit of help."

"It's not really up to me. I mean, this place isn't mine. I'd have to talk to Mrs. Rockshaw." Hugh paused as he thought about Jack's return and the family crisis looming like a storm just days away. He shifted uneasily. "I'll talk to the Rockshaws. Tonight. I'll do it tonight. Maybe we can do some work after coffee."

Jonah's face became radiant.

• • •

Kate had tried to call him. Hugh was about to step from one frame of his life back into another. And then she had written an e-mail. She was excited he was returning to London. She had missed him hiding away like he had.

What had he achieved? What had this harsh six months of winter brought to his life? There must be something to show for it all, some progress.

He had driven Jonah back to St. Ives after a couple of hours. The boy was an inspiration, he had to admit, but it left him feeling all the more defeated. He would talk to Jack when he got back to London. Jonah would be an interesting link and a positive diversion from themselves and their respective crises. It took a child to show how silly they were being. He smiled at the irony of it all.

Elise would be back any minute. There would be no harm in his talking to her about the transition and the practicalities of letting the boy chip away with a family falling apart all around him. Hugh quite liked the image. Was this his legacy of the last six months?

• • •

Elise came in search of him, not the other way round. She found him standing in the barn just staring at the wreckage of the rock. And it unnerved her a little. She had wanted to offload her own troubles and was reminded that perhaps the winter had been rather disastrous for all of them really.

"Hugh?" she called gently from the door. "You okay?"

Hugh turned and looked at her.

"Oh hi. Sure. No, please. Come in. I was coming down to the house just now. Must have lost track of time. Jonah came over."

"Jonah? Really?"

Hugh stepped away from the Pieta as Elise came up to him.

"Yeah, I know."

"Why? Is there a problem? You're packed, I see."

Hugh sighed.

"No problem. Not really. I was thinking about all this. I'm sorry it didn't work out. I guess it wasn't going to. The cold and the winter and being miles away from it all weren't enough, I guess. I just can't do it. I was going to ask you a favor."

"What?"

"Jonah wants to practice on the stone. I said I'd ask you first." He shrugged. "It's not my place. Look, I'll pay for the stone to be removed after. I just thought that some good should come out of all this."

"Oh."

"It doesn't matter. It was a crazy idea. I'm sorry. Forget it."

Elise stirred herself. Her mind was clearly turning things over.

"No, no. I'm sure it will be okay. It's, it's just –"

"Jack. Everything."

"Yes."

"I'll mention it to him at the weekend."

Elise looked uncertain.

"It's all happening rather fast. I'm having trouble keeping up. You know, I've been thinking how you'll be up there discussing my future, and now this and well, I'm just supposed to sit down here like the good little woman and wait for the shit to land."

Hugh moved away.

"It's not like that." He glanced down at the holdall of tools. "Look, if you want me to just butt out of it all, that's fine. I only wanted to help. Seriously. That's all it was. You tell me what you want me to do. It's none of my business. You're right."

Elise frowned.

"There's no need to be like that. I'm just saying how I feel."

"And that's fine by me. Feel what you feel and assert your rights over . . . over whatever it is –"

"Jack's fucking affair. His midlife crisis bullshit. My rights over that."

Hugh shrugged.

"Well there you go. Look, I just thought I could help, you know, be your advocate. You don't trust me do you? I mean, you think I'll conspire with your adulterous husband. Bring down a load of shit, as you say. In that case, where there's no trust, I can't help you Elise. And that's a shame because I really want to. I've got nothing out of this last six months. Right now, I'm feeling my career is fucked. And *there's* the proof." He pointed at the unfinished sculpture. "I have so neglected people in my life. I've been a fanatic and through all my so-called creativity I've just left a trail of destruction. If I could glean some small recompense, it would be to help Jonah and you."

Elise didn't answer.

"Mum? Mum?" Simon was calling from the house. The voice made them both stir and disengage.

"Better go. Jack said he'd phone. Can we talk after dinner?"

"Sure." Hugh bent down and started to busy himself with the bag.

"Will you leave the tools?" Elise asked, beginning to walk away.

"We'll see. Let's just leave it. I'll be down later."

"Okay," Elise said softly.

29

The train rolled slowly through west London rocking gently from side to side against the points and curving past the butt ends of Paddington's cheap hotels and the urban scrawl of graffiti tags. London was a cruel and unrelenting city of the mind. You didn't arrive. You were consumed. Five minutes to go and people were already standing in the aisle of his carriage as if their moronic impetuosity would get them all there sooner or that there really was some competition to be won. Hugh closed his eyes and wondered what was happening. He had been on a journey to nowhere.

To return to a place was to erase the time since you departed. What was it that Elise had said about Odysseus going back to Ithaca? There were snippets of conversation he could remember and they floated aimlessly in his brain like motes.

The train lurched. The queue in the aisle staggered slightly, with some passengers steadying themselves; then there came the echo of whistles, train doors slamming, and the hollow low rumble of the city. Hugh sat and watched the world suck the commuters out and he waited patiently for the carriage to empty.

When they were gone and rail workers came in with their black plastic bin liners and cleaning sticks, he rose from his seat and went to collect his bags.

• • •

Jack answered his mobile. It was Hugh.

"Hi, Hugh. I just checked in . . . No it's just behind the Tate Modern . . . No, no, I'm okay for tonight. Flight was fine. Do you want to meet here? I could come over to Bermondsey . . . Yeah, sure. Okay, I'll get a taxi. It's no distance . . . Hugh? Um, thanks for doing this . . . Well, anyway, so see you at Village East. Seven sounds fine."

Jack lowered his phone and lay back on the bed. London felt safe. It was an anonymous zone between a departure and arrival. Hugh didn't worry him. Nothing Hugh would say could undo everything, could erase the last six months. He had no guilt. If anything, he needed to rally a counter offensive and show them that nothing they wanted to keep was right or valuable. But the truth was all he could think about was Amy and how she had left him like that and it had all meant so much. Though she had gone, she was still there because she hadn't said goodbye. In fact she had out maneuvered him into feeling *he* had done the bunk not her. She had left him in a state of blissful suspension. He wondered, briefly, if he was going mad.

• • •

Elise took the kids over to Gwithian for the day. The idea had been Simon's. Jonah had turned up and they had found him in the barn bent down picking over the tools Hugh had left.

"We're going surfing. Coming?" Simon announced. Jonah looked up a little startled and seemed uncomfortable and then Elise had stepped in and she sided with Simon.

"We'll pick up your board and stuff on the way."

"Surf's perfect," affirmed Simon and he moved back from the door and started to go, like there was no further need to waste time discussing things. Mrs. Rockshaw hovered.

"Let's do something just to get out of here. It'll help you, Jonah. Please will you come? It's perfect out."

Jonah rose to his feet and nodded. He seemed a little confused, as if he'd been asleep and dreaming. He glanced back at the bag and the chisel in his hand and shrugged.

"Okay. Sure, why not?" He hesitated before returning the tools reluctantly.

"You can come back here after, if you like; sleep over in the studio," said Elise, feeling a little guilty.

Jonah's eyes lit up and he smiled.

"Really? Can I?"

"Of course. It'll be fine and you can work tonight and tomorrow. It'll be good for you to get away for a bit."

"Are you coming or not?" came Simon's impatient voice from near the house. They both looked round at the open door.

"He's such a bossy boots, isn't he," said Elise smiling. "Come on. Let's go."

There was a deep swell far out beyond the bay and the March wind was bright and strong and had the waves whipped into perfect curves hooped over and driving hard onto the three-mile long stretch of beach. Every now and then, the sea would explode against the rocks of the lighthouse sending up geysers of white plumes against the mad blue sky. Elise sat back against the ridge along the base of the cliffs and she squinted for a glimpse of the boys far off in the low tide. There were few tourists and the vast expanse of sand was almost entirely their own. She could see a few black dots of surfers way down the bay toward Hayle but no one at the lighthouse end. It felt like the old days and Elise allowed herself to feel nostalgic for happier times. If only Caja had come too, it would have softened the melancholy of reminiscence a little. She wished to keep the moment forever. Where had all the restless need for change come from? What harm could come from the endless repetition of these rare days? She wondered if there was something in the moment that might lend weight to the argument of her life that would give her the strength and resolve to stand up to Jack. This was authentic and even just one of these days was enough to justify the years. She was one of the lotus-eaters and Jack was possessed by some *fleur du mal* that would drive him crazy and she would follow him. Hugh was wrong. They were all wrong. Seize the day, yes, but hold onto it.

• • •

Homme libre, toujours tu chériras la mer!
La mer est ton miroir; tu contemples ton âme
Dans le déroulement infini de sa lame,
Et ton esprit n'est pas un gouffre moins amer.

Tu te plais à plonger au sein de ton image;
Tu l'embrasses des yeux et des bras, et ton coeur
Se distrait quelquefois de sa propre rumeur
Au bruit de cette plainte indomptable et sauvage.

Vous êtes tous les deux ténébreux et discrets:
Homme, nul n'a sondé le fond de tes abîmes;
Ô mer, nul ne connaît tes richesses intimes,
Tant vous êtes jaloux de garder vos secrets!

Et cependant voilà des siècles innombrables
Que vous vous combattez sans pitié ni remords,
Tellement vous aimez le carnage et la mort,
Ô lutteurs éternels, ô frères implacables!

— Charles Baudelaire

Amy wondered if Jack knew the poem. She didn't want to come across as all naïve and full of excitement over stuff everyone else had discovered and had discarded ages ago. When she closed the book, her throat was tight with suppressed tears and anger at herself. Her pride ached. She would not write. She would not send him this dumb fucking poem and look like some lame-o that would make him laugh at her. Not yet, anyway. She had to live this hard life for some good many years before what she wanted to say would appear strong and true. Time lent gravity to feelings and so she would bury this deep down and carry it about with her like all the other crap that people carried around inside themselves waiting for the moment it might seem sincere and real. Amy sighed, laughed at herself, and wiped at her eyes.

• • •

The phone rang. Hugh knew it was Kate because in her mind she sensed he had just arrived back at his flat and she was on tenterhooks and –

"Christ!" Hugh shut the front door behind him with his foot and dropped his bags onto the floor. Maybe he should just let it ring. How many times had she tried to phone before he'd got there? The call kept ringing. She wasn't giving up.

"Hugh? You're back."

"Kate. Yes. I just literally walked through the door."

Silence.

"Can we meet up? We don't have to go out. I'll cook something here. Come over Hugh. I've missed you."

"I can't. I'm seeing Jack, Jack Rockshaw."

"I don't want to talk on the phone. I don't want to say anything like this. Even if it's the last time, I just want to talk about it. About us and . . . you know."

"Yes. I agree. Look, Kate, I've just got in. I'm fucked in the head about what's happened. I don't know where I am."

"I understand. The Pieta –"

"No." Hugh felt the anger and frustration rise. "I don't want to talk about anything."

"Oh."

"Look, I'm sorry. I'm tired. I'm fucked. You missed the show and I'm not ready just right now to explain six months of . . . shit, basically. It's not your fault. I'm just tired . . . Kate?"

"Okay. I understand. I just wanted to reconnect. I've missed you."

Kate's words left Hugh feeling confused, almost tearful. He really had just come full circle as if he thought he had discovered a route out of the forest only to end up back where he'd started.

"Kate?"

"It's okay. Give me a ring when you're ready."

"Kate? I just want you to live your life. *Your* life. Your very own life. If I knew you didn't need me like this, I'd have phoned you the minute the plane landed."

"Okay, well maybe you're in one of your moods. I'm sorry I rang."

"Don't be sorry. It's not like that. I missed you. Really. Kate?"

Hugh lowered the handset and put it back on the charger. He noticed the left messages light was blinking.

• • •

Jack Rockshaw: 'Obfuscation' 2010 - 2013 celebrates the recent work of Jack Rockshaw, Karl Lukowski associate visiting Professor of Photographic Art at Hunter College, Winter 2012 - 2013. Rockshaw is an internationally acclaimed photographer with a regular presence on both the London and New York art stages. Best known for challenging boundaries between the figurative and abstract, portrait and landscape, Rockshaw's most recent work explores the power of chiaroscuro and Rembrandt lighting effects to blend, fuse, and obscure forms that expose the conceptual impact on perception. His works vibrate before the eye. We are invited to impose our beliefs on what we see but find our perceptions radically altered by the time we manage to tear ourselves away. Rockshaw has often been cited as a Gestalt artist and, less flatteringly, an illusionist. His latest works delight less for being trompe l'oeils but more for a complexity and depth that have the viewer transfixed if not floundering. For example, his largest piece: 'Notan II' is not a perceptual game; the confusion is deeply disturbing. This contemporary retrospective exhibition provides a unique and all too rare opportunity to explore Rockshaw's contribution to fine art photography. Three works will be further exhibited at this year's Frieze Art Fair, New York in May and have been given to the college on permanent loan. Remaining works are available for purchase. A full list of works and prices are detailed in the exhibition catalogue. The exhibition ends on March 29th. Opening times are between 09.00 and 16.00 weekdays and 10.00 to 14.00 weekends. Entry is free of charge to college faculty and CUNY student body members and $5.00 visitors. Visitors should report to college visitor reception.

"Illusionist? Fucking bitch!"

30

Acts of creativity get some folks all flustered and panicky, like they feel they're supposed to voice their uninvited opinions. Look, no one's asked you to like it or hate it. It's just there. So calm down, go home, and watch TV; or do something else safe and bland with your life.

• • •

"So what will you do?"

"I don't know. I suppose I'm free aren't I. I've thought about France but it's full of French. Spain maybe?"

Jack sighed and leaned away from the table.

"It's women, isn't it?"

"Women?" Hugh frowned. Jack continued.

"The only way I'll get what I really want is to be a solitary. A hermit."

"Then do it. There's a high price to pay, mind."

Jack looked at Hugh carefully.

"*You* could do it. You've arrived. Don't become involved with any woman, Hugh. Do you get me?"

Hugh smiled.

"So tell me about Amy."

"America is two dimensional but Americans aren't. It's the only country I know where individuals are not represented by their culture.

It must be something to do with capitalism: all that marketing and promotion. What you see isn't what you get. Maybe if Amy was here she'd look pretty ordinary. Yes. I've seen that before. An exciting New Yorker comes across rather transparent in London. They don't travel well."

"So that's Amy written off."

"Not really. Actually, she rubbed me out." Jack waved his hand dismissively.

"So was it a fling? I mean, now you're back, does it all seem unreal?"

"It wasn't a fling, Hugh. I wasn't trying to prove I could still get it up. Look, can we get over this whole midlife crisis thing. It's ridiculous. Is that what Elise has been saying?"

"Not really."

"Was Kate a fling? What the fuck's a 'fling' anyway? It's another one of those ridiculous words like 'adultery' or 'affair'. No one uses these labels anymore; they're loaded with monotheistic shit. They trivialize complexity: What are you doing? Oh, you're having an affair. And there it is. And if it's an even more trivial and selfish act, we'll call it a fling. So that was easy. And I'm condemned, maybe, but I've still no idea what's going on. Language gets used to paper over like this because we're lazy and morality is lazy. Fuck judgmental language. When I choose to sleep with a woman, I'm not asking the world's opinion."

"Or your wife's."

"Ah, now wait a minute. 'Wife' what's that? Just another word. Just another imposed cultural concept that's there to tie us up and strap us down. Elise is not a wife. Elise is a woman. A human being. Sure, I went through some weird ceremony and I'll apologies for that because it was a mistake. If I loved Elise, I should have spat on marriage. My wedding was a stupid superstitious load of bollocks. Am I to be condemned for acknowledging I made that mistake? But it doesn't somehow magically change the reality, the fact that Elise is a woman and I am a man. I'll have nothing to do with all that wife and husband bullshit."

"Do you love Elise?"

"Yes."

"And hurting her doesn't matter?"

"Hogamous, higamous. The hurt is her own. I'm not saying she can't have other men. Did you sleep with her?"

"No I didn't, actually."

"That's a shame."

"Elise loves you."

"Then she's a fool. Look, if you're playing the devil's advocate, I'm the devil's defendant. Don't take me too literally, Hugh."

"I'm not."

"I'm just trying to work all this out. I don't know the answers. But I do know that morality has nothing to do with this. Ethics just muddies the water and nothing right or good ever comes out of it. I don't give a fuck about moral high grounds and all that guilt crap. It's all just power games. And on that, I *am* being serious."

"So what do we do with all the pain? It's not just Elise. What about Simon and Caja? Don't you feel bad about them?"

Jack sighed.

"Sure. I've thought about that. The hurt. Well, now, that is what it's all about . . . Listen, I'm not kicking them onto the street. I'll support them. My behavior doesn't involve acts of cruelty or even neglect. I will provide. In return, I ask them to understand that I'm a free individual. I'm independent and I must move on with my life. I invite them, by my example, to free themselves and live authentic and independent lives. If they want to judge and condemn me as some sort of sinner, let them. I genuinely don't give a shit about that side of things."

"I know."

"I've come back to talk to them. I'll not chicken out or cringe away from that. Why should I? I'm not ashamed, Hugh. I was ashamed before about how I was living a lie. Listen, my relationship with Amy doesn't trivialize anything. Not in my mind. If they want to use her in that way, let them. It doesn't bother me."

"Jack?"

"What?"

"Do you dislike Elise? Are you bored with your kids? Why are you turning your back on them? Are people to be so easily dumped?"

Jack's face fell.

"No."

"Why not take them with you? At least offer them the chance."

"Even if they could drag themselves from the endless repetition and the comfort, it would all just start again. The individual is dynamic, the group always gravitates toward stasis. The best way to keep a crowd happy is to remove all conflicts of interest; get them to do nothing. Get them on Facebook or watching cookery TV. Groups don't wander and explore, it's something individuals do. It's terrible. I mean, we're a social animal of individuals and there's always this paradox. It's a flaw in our species and it will eventually destroy us."

"You should give them the opportunity, Jack. Seriously, people do it. Tell them there's going to be a revolution. Sell up, move to, I don't know, Greece or somewhere. Have an open marriage, an open life. Show them how to live, Jack. Your mission can be theirs if you're willing to lead them."

"If they're willing to follow. Sure, I'll think about it. Why not? And if they laugh at me or think I'm mad?"

"Then let them. At least you tried. Later in their lives, they'll realize you were right."

"Maybe."

• • •

From his window, he could see the dark blue of the high water in the harbor. The fishing boats were returning with their silver catches of sea bream and mullet. The sun warmed the pink tower of Notre-Dame-Des-Anges. From the terrace below rose threads of rich brown coffee and the tinkling of breakfast things being placed upon the table. It was barely spring but already the day glowed warmth and the sparrows were restless along the red walls.

"*Michel? Es-tu là?*"

"*Oui. J'arrive.*"

His mother appeared below, a white cloth in her hands. She looked up at him and smiled.

"*Bonjour. Viens mon chéri. Ça va?*"

"*Maman?*"

"*Oui?*"

"Je suis heureux. Quelle belle journée. Quelle belle ville. Je veux habiter toujours ici et je ne veux plus jamais quitter."

His mother laughed and shrugged then turned away. He lost sight of her beyond the wall.

"*Donc nous allons rester ici*," came her voice.

He turned from the window and smiled. It wasn't the town that made him happy. It was the change in his mother. The church bells began to ring across the harbor and he was filled with a tremendous sense of stillness as if time had stopped, as if the moment was a painting of a simple bedroom and a window that looked out over the sailing boats and the ancient stones.

They breakfasted alone together, mother and son. And they talked about the things they would do in the day ahead. They talked of Paris and school and a friend who might come down to stay and books and music and the things they liked. They ate croissants and pains au chocolat.

"Mum?"

His mother looked up a little startled.

"*Oui?*"

"I had a strange dream last night."

His mother looked away and dabbed at the crumbs on her plate. She shrugged a little.

"*As-tu eu un cauchemar?*"

"No. Not really. It was about papa. But it doesn't much matter. I'm sorry."

"Michel, if you want to see him, then I can't stop you. You miss him of course."

"No. It's fine. I don't want to make you unhappy and I love the way things are. I mean here. Don't be upset maman."

• • •

It was the last Sunday in March, the day when British clocks are put forward one hour, and the day, in spite of the last wintry squalls, when spring receives some supporting recognition from the powers that be. And Sunday morning was when Hugh Borne would walk from his small flat in Bermondsey Square past St. Mary's church to the café down the street.

"You all right there?"

Hugh turned round at the voice. Friendly. Like a student working weekends.

"Sorry. Yeah. Um, I'll have a cappuccino," he replied.

"Large or regular?" It was the girl. She spoke with her back to him, already busy at the machine. Hugh hesitated and she glanced around.

"I don't know. Large, I guess."

"Large? Chocolate on top?"

"Sure. Why not. Yes, thanks."

The girl turned completely round to face him. She wiped her hand on her apron and turned a key on the register. Another machine. Her movements were automated.

"£2.89. Anything else?"

"No, that's fine.

The girl reached back for his cappuccino and lifted it round. She pushed the mug across the counter at him, avoiding eye contact.

"Thanks."

Hugh took the coffee and turned away. The window seat was still free but people were beginning to come in and he felt his legs jerk into more purposeful action. This was London: a seat free for a second then gone.

He went over and sank thankfully into the black vinyl chair. Arne Jacobson. Bloody awkward and uncomfortable. He looked at his cappuccino still miles away, like his life. He sighed inaudibly to himself. The young woman, the one who had knocked his coffee months before, was there. She'd already gone out for a cigarette. A bag of blue smoke billowed past the window and she was chatting to someone he couldn't see beyond the frame. She had her right skinny elbow cupped in her left hand, hips slouched, high arched wrist hooked over her cigarette.

He was fond of the anonymous people and he had to admit he rather liked being back. He thought about Jack. Poor tortured Jack now sitting on the train down to Cornwall trapped by his desperate desire to escape. There was definitely something restless about creativity. But things did change, albeit imperceptibly. The Hugh Borne who had sat in this chair in the autumn was not the same Hugh Borne who now sat there looking out on Sunday morning Bermondsey Street. Six months ago, he had been restless and fraught like Jack. He had returned a humbled man. He quite liked this new Hugh Borne: a little calmer, a little wiser, perhaps. For the first time, art had swung a punch back at him and had left him sprawled on the canvas. What had Sven Berlin written?

> *In the end I must leave Cornwall: the fight with the landscape and the forces there, coupled with the fight in one's own soul, was too great: that is why no one stays there: all have left as pilgrims leave a haunted city, and only in the later dreams of that experience have done great work.*

Relax it doesn't matter.

Maybe he would paint. He imagined Jonah down there in the barn right now chipping away at the old beat up rock. Maybe he'd go and visit in the summer. Maybe he wouldn't

Made in the USA
Lexington, KY
04 February 2014